Thieves in the Night

They came on the fifth night, in the dark of the moon. It was certainly no accident that they waited until they had a moonless night, Longarm figured. They came in the dead dark, sometime past midnight, he judged, and they came as quiet as they could. Which was not particularly quiet.

A small herd of elk or cattle would have made the same amount of noise. Until they decided to put on a sneak. Then, Longarm knew, an elk could make like a ghost, a will-o'-the-wisp, day or night. He had hunted elk, on stands much like this one, and knew an animal passed below him without his ever seeing or hearing it.

Not so with these fellows.

Four of them again, he judged. He wondered if they were the same four. And what their instructions were.

It is one thing to hoorah a man or to haze him out of town. It is something else entirely to commit cold-blooded, deliberate murder. What these men seemed to have in mind was, in fact, murder.

One thing was sure. If Kyle Burgen intended to move Don Carter off this land, the only way he could accomplish it would be to kill the retired Ranger . . .

TABOR EVANS

LONGARM

AND THE
NIGHT RAIDERS

JOVE BOOKS, NEW YORK

THE BERKLEY PUBLISHING GROUP
Published by the Penguin Group
Penguin Group (USA) Inc.
375 Hudson Street, New York, New York 10014, USA
Penguin Group (Canada), 90 Eglinton Avenue East, Suite 700, Toronto, Ontario M4P 2Y3, Canada
(a division of Pearson Penguin Canada Inc.)
Penguin Books Ltd., 80 Strand, London WC2R 0RL, England
Penguin Group Ireland, 25 St. Stephen's Green, Dublin 2, Ireland (a division of Penguin Books Ltd.)
Penguin Group (Australia), 250 Camberwell Road, Camberwell, Victoria 3124, Australia
(a division of Pearson Australia Group Pty. Ltd.)
Penguin Books India Pvt. Ltd., 11 Community Centre, Panchsheel Park, New Delhi—110 017, India
Penguin Group (NZ), 67 Apollo Drive, Rosedale, Auckland 0632, New Zealand
(a division of Pearson New Zealand Ltd.)
Penguin Books (South Africa) (Pty.) Ltd., 24 Sturdee Avenue, Rosebank, Johannesburg 2196,
South Africa

Penguin Books Ltd., Registered Offices: 80 Strand, London WC2R 0RL, England

This is a work of fiction. Names, characters, places, and incidents either are the product of the author's imagination or are used fictitiously, and any resemblance to actual persons, living or dead, business establishments, events, or locales is entirely coincidental

LONGARM AND THE NIGHT RAIDERS

A Jove Book / published by arrangement with the author

PRINTING HISTORY
Jove edition / April 2012

Copyright © 2012 by Penguin Group (USA) Inc.
Cover illustration by Milo Sinovcic.

ISBN: 978-0-515-15057-5

JOVE®
Jove Books are published by The Berkley Publishing Group,
a division of Penguin Group (USA) Inc.,
375 Hudson Street, New York, New York 10014.
JOVE® is a registered trademark of Penguin Group (USA) Inc.
The "J" design is a trademark of Penguin Group (USA) Inc.

PRINTED IN THE UNITED STATES OF AMERICA

10 9 8 7 6 5 4 3 2 1

Chapter 1

U.S. Marshal William Vail's expression was . . . different. The normally confident lawman seemed uncertain. Worried, his top deputy thought.

Longarm—Deputy Marshal Custis Long—leaned forward and accepted the plump panatela Billy Vail handed him. That too was unusual.

"Would you like something to drink?" the boss asked from behind his broad desk.

"No, I don't think so."

"I don't mean wine this time. I know you don't much care for wine," Billy said. "I mean a real drink. I have a bottle of rye here."

Longarm's interest perked up. Then he became suspicious. He bit the twist off the tip of his cigar and spit it into his hand, half stood, and leaned forward to accept the light Billy offered. "I could use a taste." He settled back onto his chair and puffed gently on the excellent cigar.

Billy stood and went to the cabinet on the side wall of his office in Denver's Federal Building. He brought out a bottle of rye—Longarm recognized the label; it was a good brand, expensive—and poured a generous measure, then handed the glass to Longarm.

It was about half past ten on a Monday morning, and Billy definitely was not one to be offering whiskey at that hour. Moreover, when the boss was in an expansive mood and might want to offer a man a decent drink, it was normally bourbon, which he himself favored, and not Longarm's preferred rye. Something was up here. The cigar and the whiskey were good though.

"Here's to you, Boss." Longarm saluted the former Texas Ranger with an upraised glass.

Billy returned to his chair and sat, sunlight reflecting off his bald pate, concern pulling at his face. "Custis, I have a favor to ask of you."

Longarm leaned forward in his chair. "Hell, is that all, Boss? Whatever 'tis, you know I'll do 'er." He meant that too. Billy Vail had been damned good to him. He would walk through fire for the man. And there had not been all that many men encountered throughout Longarm's life that he could honestly say that about.

"Don't be so quick to make any promises, Custis. This has nothing to do with the law. Nothing to do with this office. I want . . . I need . . . a favor. And understand, please. I'll not hold it against you if you would rather not do it."

"I already told you, Billy. Whatever 'tis, I'll do it. For you."

"We'll see," Vail said. He leaned back in his chair, swiveled around, and stared out of the window for a few moments. Longarm did not know what the boss was seeing out there, but he did not think it had anything to do with the view.

Billy turned his chair to face Longarm again. "You know I used to be a Texas Ranger."

Longarm nodded. That was not exactly news Billy was telling him.

"Back then, riding for the Frontier Battalion, I made some dear friends. Friends dearer to me than life itself." He spun his chair around again and coughed into his fist in a vain attempt to hide the emotion that suddenly overwhelmed him. Then again he turned to face Longarm. "One of those friends is in trouble now. At least I think he is, based on some things I've heard. He is not the sort of man who would come right out and ask for help. If anything, he is a prickly son of a bitch. But I would do anything in this world for him, as I know he would for me as well."

"You're lucky," Longarm said. "To have a pard like that, well, it don't happen to a man all that often. Reckon we oughta hang on to a friend like that whenever we go an' find one."

"Exactly," Billy said, nodding. "That is the sort of friend Don Carter is to me. And now that he needs me, I find that I can do nothing to help him."

Longarm took a swallow of his rye but otherwise clamped his mouth shut. He had said what he had to say. Now he wanted to listen.

"You know that my wife is about to have a surgery for . . . well, I shouldn't be saying what it is for. She would not approve of me talking about it."

Longarm nodded. He indeed did know about Mrs. Vail's surgery. The boss's clerk, Henry, had told him. It was an unmentionable female thing, and Longarm had no desire to hear any specifics about it. But it was a serious thing. He did know that much.

"I can't leave her, Custis." Billy's face twisted for a second, then took on a stony poker expression. "I simply cannot do that. She has to come before Don."

"Yes, sir, of course." Longarm finished his rye and leaned forward to place the glass on Billy's desk.

"Refill?"

Longarm shook his head. "No, sir. Thank you."

"You don't know Don. Not many do. Like I said, he is prickly. He hides himself behind a . . . Well, truthfully, he hides behind a rather unpleasant façade. It took me three years to see behind that exterior to the real man, but when

I did, I came to love him as my brother. And now that he needs me, I can't leave Denver. Surely you understand that. I have to be here for my wife and I cannot go to Don now."

"I understand that well enough, Boss." Longarm smiled. "If you like, I'll go down there an' see to things for you."

"Would you?" Billy stood and began to pace back and forth on the far side of his desk. "I hate to ask it of you. And it would not be official business. I couldn't authorize that. It would be vacation time, not official duty. Naturally I would reimburse you for any expenses you incur. I would make sure you wouldn't be out anything but your time."

"Hell, Boss, after all you done for me, you an' your lady too, you don't need to reimburse nothing. I'm just glad to help any which way that I can. Now, tell me where this Don Carter fella is an' what I can do for him."

Chapter 2

Longarm packed—a matter of but a few minutes any time and even less for this trip, as he intended to bring very little with him—and took a hansom to the Denver & Rio Grande depot. He paid the driver and went inside to check on the timetable, although he would have thought he should have it memorized by now.

He reached for his vest pocket to check the departure against the current time, only to remember well after his hand was already on its way that at the moment he had neither his vest nor his Ingersoll pocket watch. He looked at the big regulator wall clock instead.

Five and a half hours until his southbound pulled out, he saw with a grunt. Five and a half hours to kill.

Longarm grunted again. But with a grin included this time. He went to the ticket agent's booth.

"Afternoon, Frank."

The clerk smiled. "Good afternoon yourself, Marshal. What can I do for you today?"

"I need for you to hold my bag behind the counter for a spell, Frank. I'm early and don't want to drag the thing around with me till it's time for my train. Can you do that for me?"

"Surest thing, Marshal. I'll be glad to. Just come through the gate there and set it down. I'll see that no one bothers it."

"Thanks, Frank, you're a pal." Longarm deposited his carpetbag behind the counter, thanked the ticket agent again, and was whistling on his way out of the depot.

He walked east four blocks to one of Denver's more exclusive—that is, expensive—restaurants. McQueen's Chop House was only open for supper, but at this early afternoon hour the staff would be on duty, starting fires in the stoves and ovens, laying place settings on the tables, and making sure the dining room was immaculate from floor to ceiling. Diners at McQueen's paid for, and received, nothing but the best.

Longarm went around to the side and entered an alley there, having to squeeze past a heavy dray unloading crates of . . . something he did not see what.

Longarm stepped aside while a workman with a large crate on his shoulders went inside, then he followed close behind him. The head chef was personally in charge of the deliveries. He nodded to Longarm but gave his attention to the thick-set workman and the man's load.

Longarm waved to the chef and went through the kitchen into the dark, empty dining room. A pair of waiters, not yet in uniform, were busy setting up the tables.

"Where's Jenny?" Longarm asked the nearer of them.

The man paused in his work to give Longarm a curt nod and to incline his head to the right, toward the doorway.

Longarm followed the direction to the lobby, where Jenny Littleboro was fussing with the menu folders, placing handwritten "Specials of the Day" notices in with the printed menus.

The girl beamed with pleasure when she saw Longarm. "What a wonderful surprise," she said, raising her cheek for a discreet kiss. "To what do I owe the honor?"

"Nothin' good, I'm afraid. Our picnic for this weekend is gonna be put off till I get back."

Her joyful expression turned to one of sorrow. "You're leaving?"

"Ayuh, I'm afraid so." He smiled and said, "It's only postponed though. We'll go for certain sure soon as I get back."

"Where are you going this time?"

"Arizona," he said. "I'm waitin' on the next southbound right now. Got a little time to spare an' wanted to come tell you myself instead o' sending you a note."

Jenny frowned. "Arizona? It's hot down there."

Longarm laughed. "Darlin', it's hot up here right now."

"Yes, but up here it's a *nice* hot." The girl sighed. "I'll miss you, Custis."

"I'll miss you too, darlin'."

"Do you have a few minutes?"

"Sure."

"Come with me." Jenny linked her arm with his and guided him toward the shuttered cloakroom where in a few hours Lucille, the hatcheck girl, would be holding forth.

They were an odd couple, Longarm tall and swarthy, and Jenny a petite blonde who looked small enough to fit into his pocket. She was cute and lively and full of pep, however. And she loved to fuck. One of her more endearing traits, in his opinion.

He raised an eyebrow as they reached the closed door into the cloakroom.

Jenny laughed. "Trust me."

"Always," he said, and followed as she entered the cloakroom and closed the door behind them.

Jenny pressed a finger against her lips to request silence. Longarm winked at her.

The pretty girl lifted herself onto tiptoes and offered her lips for a proper kiss, her mouth open and tongue probing. Her breath tasted of peppermint.

"Now that's . . . ," he began, only for Jenny to cut him off with an abrupt "Shh" and a glance toward the door.

There was not so much as a latch to hold the door closed, and he could hear the waiters chattering only a few steps away from the open archway between the dining room and the lobby.

She returned to kissing him while at the same time her right hand began massaging the front of his trousers. Longarm's response was immediate. And powerful. His dick sprang instantly to attention, bulging the front of his britches so hard he worried that the buttons might pop off.

Jenny leaned back and grinned, once again shushing him with a finger placed against her pretty lips.

She giggled. And dropped to her knees in front of him.

The girl's fingers worked deftly to slip the buttons of his fly out of their holes. She reached inside, found the hard, fleshy shaft, and pulled it out of his pants.

Jenny licked him, her tongue running up his shaft and down again to his balls. She peeled back his foreskin and ran her tongue around and around the head of his cock.

She dropped a stream of spit onto the head and worked the foreskin up and down while she fondled and licked his balls for several delightful seconds, then she stood, turned around to face the other way and lifted the skirt of her very conservative uniform.

She was not wearing anything beneath the full skirt, and she giggled again as she bent over the hatcheck girl's empty counter and pushed her bare, pink, round little ass toward him.

Her hint was not exactly subtle. Longarm was smiling as he stepped forward, bent his knees to get down to Jenny's level, and rammed his now wet and decidedly ready cock into the girl's accommodating flesh.

She was a small girl, but she took everything he could give her, the wet heat of her surrounding his dick and clenching it tight.

He could feel the sharp contractions of her body as she came, and then came again.

Longarm felt his own sap very quickly rising.

He glanced to his right in response to movement seen out of the corner of his eye.

A waiter pushed the door open, on his way into the cloakroom on some errand or other. The fellow saw Longarm and Jenny locked together like that, she bent over the counter and he hunched over her bare ass with his dick stuffed up her cunt.

The waiter's eyes went wide. Then he grinned and gave Longarm a thumbs-up before withdrawing as silently as he had arrived.

Longarm silently laughed, shrugged, and went back to what he had been doing.

Chapter 3

The Custis Long who stepped down off the stagecoach in Good Hope, Arizona, looked very little like the Longarm who lived and worked in Denver, Colorado. This man wore a tattered, black broadcloth coat, faded denim bib overalls, scuffed brown boots, and a very dirty snuff brown Stetson that looked like it had seen better days. He had no shirt behind the bib of his overalls, just the red flannel of old longjohns.

His only luggage was a battered and travel-worn carpetbag. He needed a bath and a shave and looked like he could use a stiff drink as well . . . but could not afford any of those.

This Custis Long turned to the nearest saloon and headed immediately for the flyspecked offerings on the free lunch spread. He grabbed a pickled quail egg and a chunk of dry, stale bread and crammed them into his mouth like he had not eaten in days.

"Say, bub, that food is for paying customers," the bartender warned, his hand hovering over a bung starter. "I don't see any of your money on the bar."

"Sorry. Sorry," Longarm said, bread crumbs spraying from his lips. "Sorry," he said again. "Beer, please."

"You got money to pay for a beer?"

"Yes. I . . . uh, I do." He dug into a pocket and came out with some loose change, most of which appeared to be pennies. Longarm slowly and carefully counted out ten pennies and laid them on the bar. "Is that enough?" he asked.

The barkeep held his hand palm upward and motioned with his fingers for the pennies to keep on coming. "Three more."

"Three?"

The bartender nodded. "Three. Or you can lay down two bits and get two drinks. That makes it only twelve and a half cents. You want two drinks for a quarter?"

Longarm shook his head and pushed the three pennies across the bar with the others. "There," he said as if the amount were an accomplishment.

The bartender grunted and almost reluctantly pulled the tap to draw a beer. He set the mug down and turned away in search of something more interesting than this drifter.

Custis Long buried his mustache in the suds and took a long, thirsty pull at the beer, then returned his attention to the free lunch platter. He ate like a man who had been hungry for days.

Chapter 4

Damn you, Billy, Longarm thought to himself as he walked away from the saloon. What he wanted now, what he needed now, was a hot bath to wash away two days' worth of railroad soot and travel grime.

Under ordinary circumstances he could just flop his badge out for a hotel clerk and fill out a voucher for the hotel to get paid by the government. Or if necessary he could easily afford to pay for such out of his own pocket. That was ordinarily. This trip was not ordinary.

Billy said this Don Carter fellow was prickly. And proud. Too proud to accept help from a deputy United States marshal who rode for Carter's old pal Billy Vail.

Hell, Billy said, the old fart might not even accept help from Billy himself.

But despite his always foul disposition, Don Carter was a sucker for a sob story. He would give his last dime to put food into a stranger's belly. That, Billy said, was the way to get close to the man. And to find out what his problem was. Or problems; there might well be a heap of them piled on the old Ranger's head.

"Find out," Billy said, "and report back to me with whatever Don's situation is. Hopefully by then my wife will be out of danger and I can afford the time away from her for a few days. All I'm really wanting you to do, Custis, is to be my eyes and ears down there. I'd prefer to go myself, but," the boss spread his hands wide, "but a man has no choice sometimes. We do what we must."

"Don't you be worryin' 'bout a thing," Longarm had assured his boss—and friend—"I'll take care of whatever it is."

"I don't want you putting yourself in danger," Billy said. "Just find out the problem and let me know. If it is only Don's financial situation, tell me that too, and I can send him whatever he needs. If I have to go into debt to square things for him, I will. Don would do almost anything for me, and I will do no less for him."

Longarm needed to think for only a moment before he smiled. "You say the man's a pushover for a sad tale an' a empty belly? Don't you be worryin' about a thing, Boss. I know just how t'get close to him."

That conversation had taken place in Denver with a bottle of excellent rye whiskey on Billy's desk and a fair amount of its contents having been transferred into Longarm's belly.

Things looked a mite different down here in Good Hope, Arizona.

Longarm headed for the biggest mercantile in sight. All Billy had been able to tell him about Don Carter's whereabouts was that he lived in Good Hope, and Longarm needed more information than that before he could find Carter and go into the act he had decided upon back there in Denver.

Chapter 5

A nondescript black-and-white cur came panting out of the alley mouth beside the general store. Longarm wondered for a moment if the dog was hostile, but it wagged its tail and dropped its head. He paused and leaned down to give the animal a pat and scratch it behind the ears.

"Get away, you son of a bitch."

Longarm looked up to see a large man with a very foul expression on his unshaven face. The fellow stood at least as tall as Longarm and was probably thirty pounds heavier, not all of it fat. He wore a knitted cloth cap, a flannel shirt, faded jeans, and steel-toe boots. He did not look happy.

"Are you talkin' to me?" Longarm asked.

"Damn right I am. You're trying to steal my dog, you bastard."

"Mister, I just . . ."

"Don't give me no shit. Just get away from the dog."

Longarm looked down at the cur and, with a shrug, gave it a final pat. "Sorry, little fella, but your owner says no, so that's that."

The dog wagged its tail and moved to follow when Longarm turned away toward the steps leading onto the general store's porch.

That should have been the end of it, but the big fellow with the belligerent attitude was not willing to let it go. With a snarl and a curse, he charged, swinging a very large fist when he did so.

"Hey now," Longarm grunted as he ducked under the first wild swing. "There ain't no call for that."

The man responded by trying to kick Longarm in the knee.

"That's enough out o' you, mister." Longarm threw a right aimed at the man's jaw, but the blow was blocked. The fellow again tried to deliver a kick.

"Can't say as I like the way you fight, asshole," Longarm said. He moved in too close to be kicked, at least not with any power behind it, and pummeled the pugnacious bastard with a series of fast, low shots to his belly.

Those made the man double over as the breath was driven out of him, and that put the fellow in perfect position for Longarm to deliver a short, vicious uppercut that landed square on the man's face. Longarm could hear the crunch of breaking cartilage, and blood spurted, flooding down over the fellow's shirt.

The black-and-white dog was jumping and whining, obviously distressed by this exchange.

The animal's owner dropped to his knees and grabbed a handkerchief from a pocket to stanch the blood, which seemed to be interfering with his breathing.

Longarm leaned down and petted the dog to calm its whining. "Sorry, little fella. You deserve better'n him."

The dog wagged its tail and followed when Longarm mounted the porch and went inside the Good Hope mercantile.

The proprietor was busy with a pair of chattering women who could not decide on the bolt of cloth they wanted, so Longarm idled through the shelves, for no good reason touching each item as he came to it.

He was debating with himself whether his feigned poverty would allow him to purchase a cigar. He loved them, but they were expensive. Because of that he had brought only a few, and those were stashed out of sight in his carpetbag. It would not do for a near-penniless drifter to be seen smoking an expensive cigar. He could probably get away with a pipe and cheap tobacco, and he had those in the carpetbag too.

The ladies finally made up their minds and triumphantly bore the bolt of chosen cloth off to the dressmaker. Longarm started toward the counter, where the storekeeper was finally free.

"There's the son of a bitch," he heard from the doorway.

Longarm turned around to see the big man with the dog—and with the rather nasty habit of kicking—standing in the doorway with a smaller and much better dressed fellow. That one was wearing a badge pinned to the lapel of his coat. He was tall and slender and looked to be about fifty years of age.

Behind the dog's owner stood two more who looked like slightly smaller versions of him. His brothers, perhaps, or coworkers. They looked like brawlers, and Longarm could guess what their purpose in being there was.

"Now what?" Longarm grumbled.

The town marshal, or whatever they called the local law in Good Hope, withdrew a revolver from a shoulder holster that had been concealed by the coat.

The gun was a no-nonsense Webley .455. A slug from one of those would be enough to ruin a man's whole day.

The Webley was pointed in Longarm's direction.

Unnerving, he thought. Decidedly so.

The lawman holding the pistol followed the direction of his revolver and approached Longarm.

"I'm Marshal Heath Stonecipher, young fellow, and I am placing you under arrest."

The big man and his pals crowded nearer, and the dog began to whine again.

"Don't give me any trouble now," Stonecipher warned.

Longarm had to make a quick decision. He could announce himself as a deputy United States marshal and walk away. Or he could keep his mouth shut about that little detail and get on with the job of helping Billy Vail's old Ranger partner.

"All right, sir. May I ask what the charge would be?"

"Fighting in public," Stonecipher said. "Max says you attacked him."

Longarm raised an eyebrow. "He says that, does he? As it happens, I say that he attacked me. I bent down to pet his dog. He didn't like that. Accused me of tryin' to steal the animal."

The dog, perhaps sensing that it was the subject of discussion here, stopped whining and lifted a paw to scratch at Longarm's pant leg. Longarm transferred his carpetbag to his other hand and ruffled the dog's ears and the back of its neck.

"He's lying, Stony. You can see that, can't you? The son of a bitch is lying."

Stonecipher grunted. He also put the Webley back under his coat. Instead he pulled out a pair of handcuffs. "Turn around, son."

"Yes, sir." Longarm hefted the carpetbag and said, "What about this?"

"Set it down. After I get the cuffs in place, I'll hand it to you," Stonecipher said.

The man named Max looked disappointed to see that the marshal would not be inflicting any violence on Longarm. He turned and motioned to his compadres, who slunk away now that they were not needed to back up their pal in a fight.

Longarm turned and offered his wrists behind his back. He felt the chill of steel as Stonecipher snapped the handcuffs around his wrists. Not too tight, though, he noticed. The marshal was being careful but not cruel, and that might well be an indication of what sort of man he was.

A few seconds later he felt the familiar grips of the carpetbag being placed in his hands.

"Come along, please, mister. Maxwell, I don't need you now, but you be before Judge Lowry first thing tomorrow morning to tell him your tale of woe."

Max stepped up close to Longarm and for a moment looked like he would throw a sucker punch now that Longarm could not defend himself. He stopped, though, when he saw the look in Longarm's eyes. And from off to the side Stonecipher growled, "Don't even think about it, Maxwell."

Max turned away in triumph and strode briskly out of the mercantile, the dog at his heels.

"Come along with me now, mister. You won't be too uncomfortable tonight. Our hoosegow bunks have springs in 'em, and my wife is a fine cook."

Stonecipher took Longarm by the elbow and guided him out onto the street.

Chapter 6

"You have a nice little jail here, Marshal," Longarm said. He meant it too. The Good Hope jail was small but tidy. There were three cells set along the back wall, a desk in the center of the room, a cot along one side wall, shelves, and a gun rack along the other. Someone, presumably Mrs. Stonecipher, had hung drapes at the large window that fronted onto the street.

"Well acquainted with jails are you, mister?" the marshal asked.

Longarm laughed. "Here an' there." Better acquainted with jails—and with the law—than Stonecipher knew, he was thinking.

"Let me take that bag of yours," Stonecipher said. "I'll set it over here in the corner. No one will bother it."

Longarm felt the carpetbag being lifted out of his hands. He waited while the marshal disposed of the bag.

"Step inside a cell. Your choice which one; it doesn't matter to me," the marshal instructed.

For no particular reason Longarm chose the cell on the left-hand wall. All of them looked clean. There was even a rough woolen blanket neatly folded on the foot of each bunk and plump mattress ticking covering the base of each. A heavy crockery thunder mug sat beneath each bunk.

"No pillows?" Longarm asked, his voice light. Stonecipher ignored him.

The cell door clanged shut behind Longarm, and Stonecipher said, "Back up to the bars so I can reach your wrists. I'll unlock those bracelets so you'll be more comfortable."

Longarm did as the man said. Stonecipher unlocked the steel around first his left wrist and then the right. Longarm turned, rubbing his wrists as he did so. "You're right, Marshal. This is much better. Thanks."

"Always glad to be of service," the man said, not meaning a bit of it. But he did seem a fair sort. Longarm liked him.

"For the record, Marshal, I was telling you the truth. I petted that dog an' the man jumped me. No reason for it that I can see."

"Maxwell likes to fight. Likes to win too, and usually does," Stonecipher said. "I can't think of a man in these parts that he hasn't whipped one time or another. My guess is that he'll keep coming at you until he beats you too."

Longarm laughed. "Then he'd best learn something about fighting. He doesn't do it very well. Mostly kicks. Leastways that's what I saw today."

"You were lucky." Stonecipher paused. "Or perhaps you're good. You say you are familiar with jails. Would that familiarity extend to fighting as well?"

Longarm grinned. "I been in a tussle now an' then."

"Professionally?"

"Oh, hell no." Longarm shook his head.

The marshal went to his desk and tossed the cell keys into his top right-hand drawer. He sat down, opened another drawer, and pulled out a ledger book, then opened it and picked up a pen. He brought an ink bottle out of yet another drawer, uncapped the bottle, and set it by the top of his ledger book. He dipped the nib into the ink and wrote something in the book, then looked over at Longarm and asked, "Name?"

"Short," Longarm said. "Custis Short." There was just the smallest chance that Heath Stonecipher or, when Longarm found him, Don Carter might have heard of a deputy U.S. marshal named Custis Long. There seemed no reason to take even that small chance of discovery.

"How do you spell Custis?" the marshal asked.

Longarm told him, and Stonecipher wrote it in his book. He carefully put the cap back on his ink bottle, wiped the nib of his pen, and put it away, then blotted the ledger and returned it to the drawer.

Stonecipher stood. "Is there anything you need?"

"No, sir, I reckon not."

The marshal nodded. "There's a water bucket and dipper on the wall beside you there. You can reach through the bars to get to it. Mind that if you make any mess, you'll have to clean it. I don't stand for any foolishness, but I go easy on a man who acts decent. I'll be back to check on you around dinnertime." Stonecipher took his hat down from the rack beside the door, put it on, and left.

Longarm shrugged. For lack of anything better to do, he lay down on the bunk that was provided, wadded the blanket up and used that as a pillow, then put his hat over his eyes. There was no sense worrying about any of this; there was nothing he could do about it.

He put his current situation out of mind and went to sleep.

Chapter 7

"Sheriff, I heard . . ."

"Marshal," Stonecipher interrupted.

"Come again?"

"Marshal. I'm town marshal of Good Hope. The county sheriff is an elected position. He'd be awfully put out to think I had my eye on his job. So you can call me 'marshal' or mister or Heath or mostly whatever you like. But all I am is a town employee, not the sheriff of this county."

"Sorry," Longarm said. He knew the difference perfectly well, of course, but he suspected that most men did not. And did not much give a shit either.

"What were you saying, son?"

"Oh, right. I was gonna say two things. One is that your fine lady is a helluva good cook. That stew was about the best I can remember having in ever so long." The comment was not a stretch. He really had enjoyed the supper Stonecipher brought him. There was even plenty of it, which was rare for a small town jail.

Stonecipher nodded. "And the other thing you wanted to ask?"

"Oh, that. Right." Longarm yawned and scratched his left armpit. He wasn't sure but that he had picked up a louse or two, which was carrying this playacting at being a bum about one step too damn far. "I heard it around that there's a fella here as has a soft spot for a hungry man. Name of Carter, I think. Don, maybe, though I ain't so sure 'bout the first name. Anyway, I heard it said a man could find a meal with this Carter fella. Would you know where I might find him?"

"You're hungry again already, Short?" Stonecipher returned.

"Aw, you know better'n that, Sher—uh . . . Marshal. I'm thinkin' about after I get outa this fine jail o' yours." He grinned. "Which I hope will be soon."

"You could look for work, you know. You seem a decent enough sort, Short. I might even help you find something. I know a man who's building a shed. He might could use some help swinging a hammer."

"Why, Marshal," he said with a laugh and another grin, "work is ag'in my principles, so thank ya but no thank ya."

Stonecipher's friendly expression faded to a scowl at this bum's unwillingness to undertake honest labor. Which was exactly what Longarm intended. If there was anything he did *not* want at the moment it was to be given a job other than that of helping Billy Vail's friend. Stonecipher's charitable impulse was nice but not welcome.

"Suit yourself," Stonecipher said coldly.

"So," Longarm said, "can you tell me where t'find this Carter fella? Please?"

Stonecipher grunted and frowned. But he gave Longarm directions to Carter's place. "He has some sort of mine up there, I think. It is out of my jurisdiction, so I don't pay it much mind, but I hear that is what he is doing."

"What sort of man is he?" Longarm asked.

Stonecipher ignored the question and turned away to rummage through some papers on his desk.

Longarm yawned again. And returned to his bunk, there not being anything better to do with his time behind bars.

Chapter 8

Municipal Court Judge Edward Lowry's gavel crashed down with conviction. Longarm winced at the noise.

Unlike many small towns, most even, Good Hope, Arizona, had an actual courtroom in an actual town hall. Both were small and unpretentious affairs, but Longarm had seen much worse. Good Hope's civic facilities were next door to the marshal's office . . . and jail.

"Time served," Lowry declared, his eyes fixed on the bum standing in front of him. "My recommendation to you, young man," said the judge, who was probably younger than Longarm, "my recommendation to you is for you to shake the dust of Good Hope from your shoes. Stony tells me you have no interest in the labor that sustains a man, so go and do your panhandling somewhere else. We don't need your kind in our community. That is a suggestion, by the way, not a judicial order. But I hope I make myself clear."

"You do, Your Honor," Longarm said contritely. "I don't want to cause trouble for no man."

Lowry cleared his throat and scowled, but he shifted sideways in his chair and on the whole seemed satisfied that his message had been delivered. The judge lifted his gaze past Longarm, to Max Jeffords, and said, "As for you,

Maxwell, I am weary of seeing you involved in common brawling. Tired of you as a witness and tired of you as a defendant standing before me. See to it that you stay out of trouble from here on or you will be spending some time behind Marshal Stonecipher's bars. Do we understand each other?"

As far as Longarm could tell the instruction made no impression on Jeffords. If he had even bothered paying attention. Longarm suspected it was a warning that held no teeth and would not be heeded in any case.

"You are free to go, young man. Marshal Stonecipher will return your possessions at your mutual convenience."

"Yes, sir, Your Honor. Thank you." Longarm turned and held his wrists out to Stonecipher, who unlocked the handcuffs on them and returned the cuffs to his pocket.

As Longarm passed out of the gated area in front of the judge's raised bench, Jeffords leaned close and under his breath hissed, "Next time, asshole. Next time I'm gonna hurt you bad."

Longarm pretended not to hear. He had come here to help Billy, dammit, and Don Carter, not to fight uncouth pieces of shit like Maxwell Jeffords. All he wanted now was to reclaim his carpetbag and get out to Carter's place.

Chapter 9

It was an hour's uphill trudge to reach Don Carter's claim high on the slopes of Benton Mountain. It sat at the head of a fold in the ground. A bald chute of smooth rock extended above the valley almost to the top of the mountain, suggesting that at one time there must have been a cascade or waterfall, certainly there had been rockfalls and snow slides from time to time, but now the chute was dry and barren save for a very thin trickle of water that flowed from somewhere on the mountainside above.

The narrow valley was wooded at its upper reaches. Lower on the mountainside mixed grasses and wildflowers covered both sides of the valley floor.

Carter had built a small, tightly constructed cabin on the northern slope, close to a stand of aspen. He had built using materials that were close to hand, and Longarm had to wonder if this friend of Billy's knew that aspen logs are notorious for warping out of shape as they age and dry out. Aspen is a poor choice as a building material. Besides, when dry, it is as easily flammable as tinder.

But then, he reasoned, maybe Carter had no intention of remaining here for any serious length of time. Perhaps

Billy's friend intended to cut and run whenever his problem, whatever it might be, was past.

As Longarm came closer, he could see a dark, empty maw dug into the rock wall at the base of the chute and spreading across the floor, almost hidden within the stands of aspen. He could see the broken scree that had been taken out of the ground to form that opening. So Carter had himself a mine of some sort here, although of course there was no way to tell what was being mined just from looking at a distance.

Longarm stopped for a breather, and automatically his hand moved to his left-side breast pocket for a cheroot.

Except he had no cheroots. And in fact had no left-side breast pocket either. Not in these rather ragged and wash-worn overalls and shabby broadcloth coat.

He was, after all, supposed to be broke. A man in his position would not have money to waste on expensive cigars. A little cigarette tobacco, perhaps, even pipe and tobacco, but not cigars.

Longarm sighed and rolled his eyes. The next chance he got, he would have to break out some of the money he had hidden and at least buy himself some tobacco. It was one thing to play a part for Billy's sake, but a man could not be expected to give up tobacco completely.

With another sigh—and a cramp in his left leg—he continued the hike up to Don Carter's mine.

Chapter 10

"Mister. Hallo the house," Longarm called loudly well before he reached the shack. Simply walking up to someone's place could get a man shot. Especially so when the place was the workings of a mine. Folks tend to get touchy where mines and money are concerned.

"Hallo?"

He received no answer from inside the shack, so Longarm chose the bole of a good-sized aspen, sat down, and leaned against it. He sat with his knees drawn up and arms wrapped around them and waited more or less patiently. Either Don Carter was not at home or, more likely, he was inside his mine and could not hear. Longarm knew better than to go poking around in there looking for the man. He would come out or he would not, but either way Longarm was not going inside looking for him.

Again he reached for a cheroot, except his smokes were waiting for him back in Denver, so he cussed a little. And waited some more.

Toward evening he heard the rattle of trace chains coming up the path from Good Hope. He stood, his knee joints cracking audibly, and turned to see a wagon coming up the mountain. The wagon was heavily built, narrow and stout.

It was pulled by two heavy-bodied sorrel cobs, each of which probably weighed the best part of a ton.

The driver was a small man with a ruddy complexion and more gray than black in his hair and mustache.

Longarm contained a smile, thinking that at least this former Ranger still had hair. His pal Billy Vail was fresh out of that commodity.

Carter wore a clean white shirt buttoned to the throat, matching coat and trousers in some dark brown material, and low-heeled boots. And if the grips were anything to go by, he carried one of the large-caliber Smith & Wesson revolvers in a cross-draw rig much like the one Longarm had tucked away in the bottom of his carpetbag.

Longarm removed his hat when the wagon came near.

"Who would you be?" Carter challenged after he stopped his horses.

Longarm bobbed his head obsequiously and said, "My name is Custis Short, sir. Would you be Mr. Cotter?"

"The name is Carter, not Cotter."

"Well, sir, a fellow along the road told me if I got around this way I should look for this Cotter fellow. Or Carter. Sorry. Anyway, he said a man might find a meal here. Maybe a couple days' work too."

Carter climbed down from his perch atop the driving box. The off horse tossed its head and stamped a foot, but both animals stood steady.

Billy's friend came just about shoulder high to Longarm. He was lean as a whip and did not look like all that much, but if Billy Vail respected the man, he was as salty as need be and would have proved that time and time again over the years. Texas Rangers were not known to be soft.

"You hungry?" Carter asked.

"Yes, sir." Longarm bobbed his head again.

The little man grunted. "Help me unload here and you can eat."

Longarm smiled and said, "Yes, sir." He went around to

the back of the wagon and dropped the tailgate. The wagon bed contained a half dozen or so wooden boxes with open tops. They were filled with items such as flour and bacon, canned goods of various sorts, and mostly, sacks of dried beans.

"Careful of that little crate," Carter said of a smaller box labeled "Red Stick Dynamite." "I'll take that myself. You can set the other things inside. But don't touch anything until I get there."

"Whatever you say, sir."

Carter grabbed the box of dynamite and carried it into the mine adit. He was not out of sight for more than a few seconds, so Longarm reasoned that either the hole was not very deep or Carter stored his explosives close to the entrance.

Longarm made short work of toting the other crates inside the cramped shack, which had a sheepherder's stove at one end of the single room and a bunk at the other with a trunk placed at the foot. There were a table and two stools in the center of the room, and that was the extent of Carter's furniture. Pegs driven between the cracks of the logs served for a wardrobe.

A heavy woolen coat and a pair of canvas overalls hung from the pegs. A pair of shelves on the back wall held pans, bare metal tin plates and tin cups, and a few other utensils. A wooden box like the ones Longarm was carrying in sat beside the stove, filled with chunks of split aspen. Lacking any instructions to the contrary, Longarm piled the boxes of eatables on the floor beneath the shelves.

By the time Longarm had the boxes of supplies inside, Carter had a fire blazing in the stove and a pot of water on to boil.

"Sit," the man instructed, pointing to the stool closer to the doorway.

Longarm dropped his hat on the floor and sat.

"Who was it told you to stop here?" Carter asked.

Longarm shrugged. "He never gave me his name nor asked for mine. He was just an ordinary fellow traveling with a bindle stiff for a companion and a friendly nature. He had some flour and I had me some coffee, so between us we made a meal. We jawed for that one evening an' each went on his way."

"Where are you bound?" Carter asked.

Longarm's only answer was another shrug.

"You say you want a few days of work?"

"Yes, sir. I'd work for found. You wouldn't have t'pay me no cash money."

Carter grunted. "We'll see then," he said noncommittally. "We'll see come tomorrow."

Chapter 11

"Take the horses out into that little trap you see there and clean out their stalls. Then you can cut and split some of that aspen that I downed last year. It's over there behind the horse trap. Cut it to stove lengths and pile it against the side of the house with the other stove wood. If you can do those things without me having to stand over you every minute of the day, maybe I can use you until you get the itch to move on again," Carter said.

"Yes, sir, thank you, sir," Longarm responded.

"Before you get started, though, you can come inside and have something to eat. The porridge I put on the stove should be ready to eat now." Carter grunted. "I like to start a day with a big bowl of porridge. It fills a man's belly and keeps you warm from the inside out. Fine stuff, porridge. I favor it."

"Yes, sir." Longarm picked up an armload of split wood before he went back inside.

It was a fine morning, the sun just coming up over the distant plains. The rolling hills and valleys stretching below Don Carter's claim were a kaleidoscope of light and shadow. At this elevation there was a sharp chill in the air. Beside the narrow thread of water that ran past the cabin a pair of mule deer does minced timidly out of the aspen to drink, followed by a yearling and another fat doe.

"You want me to lead the horses out before I eat, sir?" Longarm offered.

"That would be good, yes."

Longarm did not as much care about getting the big sorrels out to graze as he did about finding an excuse to move around some. He had slept poorly on the bare floor with only a very thin blanket as both mattress and cover. It had not helped anything that Carter lay snug on his bed, snoring fit to rattle the windows . . . if there had been any windows to rattle. Now Longarm was sore, his leg muscles cramping after all the walking he had done the day before, and his shoulders and left hip aching from contact with the hard floor all night.

The things he did for Billy Vail! he thought wryly as he took down the poles that blocked access to the shed and led both big sorrels out by their halters, grateful now that he thought about it that both animals were docile.

He led them down to a small fenced area that straddled the creek. Most of the grass that had been growing inside the trap was gone now, eaten away to the ground, and he could not see any haystack. Longarm did not much care for that. Horses need more than just grain. They have to have roughage in their bellies too. Probably Carter had an answer for that; Longarm just did not know what it might be.

He secured the sorrels inside the trap and knelt beside the thin run of icy water to splash some on his face and rinse his hands before going back up to Carter's shack.

He still had no idea what the man's problem was or how he might help with it. Hopefully Don Carter would at least mention his difficulties. Otherwise, if he was closemouthed about it, Longarm would just come right out and tell him who he was and that Billy Vail had sent him.

He stepped inside the cabin, grateful for the heat put out by the sheet-metal stove, and removed his beat-up old Stetson. Carter already had two bowls of steaming oat porridge set on the table, along with coffee and a honeycomb to sweeten the porridge. Longarm had had worse meals. He dropped his hat on the floor and straddled the stool opposite Don Carter's place.

"It's my habit," Carter said, "to pray before I eat. I don't require you to join me, but I expect you to bow your head and be quiet while I pray."

"Yes, sir."

There were only a few seconds of silence before Carter said "amen" aloud and grabbed up his spoon."

"Mind if I ask you something, sir?" Longarm had finished his porridge and was enjoying another cup of coffee before he would head out to the tasks Carter set for him.

The man seemed to ponder that simple request for a moment before he answered, "All right. You can ask. It remains to be seen whether I will answer or not."

Longarm said, "It looks to me like you're minin' something here. I'm wondering what it is that has you stuck up here on this mountain."

Carter only shrugged. And drank another swallow of coffee.

Longarm finished his second cup of the morning, excused himself, and went out to start working on the chores Carter had assigned to him.

Sometime while Longarm was busy splitting stove lengths of old-growth aspen, Don Carter disappeared, presumably inside the mine. When the sun reached its zenith, Longarm laid the maul and wedges aside and went into the cabin in search of lunch. Between the vigorous work and the high altitude, he was more than ready for something to eat.

Besides, lunch gave him an excuse to rummage through the cabin to see if he could find any clues to what Billy thought was troubling the little Ranger.

He first started a fire and set a heavy, cast iron spider on the stovetop with a glop of lard in it. While he was waiting for that to turn to liquid, he took a look inside Carter's trunk.

There was no lock on the trunk, even though it had a hasp attached that could easily be secured with a simple padlock. When he opened it, he saw why that would be so.

The trunk was full of weapons: an ordinary Winchester .44-40 along with two hundred or so rounds of ammunition in that caliber; a Sharps bull barrel .45-110 and at least a hundred rounds for that; a pair of sawed-off L.C. Smith ten-gauges with brass-walled buckshot shells to go with them; a Smith & Wesson Schofield in the same .44-40 caliber as the Winchester. Judging by the contents of that trunk, Donald Carter was prepared to go to war.

But with whom? And why?

Longarm put the weapons back the way he had found them and went to check on his skillet of now hot grease. He opened a can of embalmed beef, sliced it into the skillet, and began looking around to see if he could find the makings for a pan of biscuits.

Chapter 12

"Psst. Mr. Carter," Longarm whispered into the darkness two nights later. "Wake up."

"I'm awake." The voice came quickly, betraying no heaviness of sleep. "I hear them."

Apparently Carter had been awakened by the same sounds that brought Longarm out of a deep sleep, the sounds of hoofbeats in the night.

"Three riders," Longarm said. He paused to listen, then added, "An' one other fella by hisself, off to the north o' the others." He could hear the ropes suspending the bunk creak as Carter sat up.

"A man alone to the north? I didn't catch that. Thanks."

"What d'you think somebody would be doin' at this time o' night?" Longarm asked.

"They'd be up to no damned good, I know that," Carter said. Longarm could hear the man putting his boots on and standing, stamping into the boots but trying to be quiet about it. Then he heard the clunk of the trunk lid banging against the foot of Carter's bunk.

"Can you handle a gun, Short?"

"Yes, sir. Some."

"Are you willing to? In case you're right about those

riders, I mean. If there is a fight I understand that it wouldn't
be yours. You just work here. But . . ."

"If there's a fight, I'll stand with you," Longarm said.
"But I don't have a gun."

"I have one here you can use. It's a shotgun. You don't
have to aim close with a shotgun. Just point it and pull the
trigger. You've fired shotguns before?"

"Yes, sir, I have." Longarm would have been happier with
a six-gun, especially with his own six-gun that was hidden
away in the carpetbag. But he was supposed to be a penni-
less drifter, not a deputy United States marshal.

"Take this one then. And some shells to put in your
pockets."

"Shit," Longarm said. "I'm sleepin' in my long johns.
Don't have any pockets." He was sitting up, pulling his boots
on. It was one thing to run around in the night practically
naked, but quite another thing to be doing it barefoot on the
rocky soil up here in the mountains. A man could bust a toe
that way, and that was no fun at all. Longarm knew. He had
done it a time or two before and did not want to repeat the
experience.

He felt more than saw his way to the foot of Don Carter's
bunk. Carter placed one of the ten-gauges in his hands and
a fistful of brass shells too. Longarm pushed the release
aside and opened the breech. There was the familiar, hollow
sound as the shotgun shells dropped into the twin chambers.
He closed the breech and eared both hammers back to half-
cock. He heard Carter doing the same with the other Smith.
He partially unbuttoned the front of his long johns and
pushed the spare shells inside.

He heard Carter's boots cross the floor. The man tripped
over the blankets that had been laid down to make Longarm's
bed, an obstacle the man was not accustomed to finding
there. Carter cussed a little, stumbled, and went to the door.

Starlight and the faint glow of a quarter moon lent a
little ability to see when Don Carter pulled the door open.

"You can stay out of it if there's a fight," Carter said, "but you might need to defend yourself, so stay ready. Just in case."

"The hell with that," Longarm said. "If there's gonna be a fight, I want t'be out where I can move around. Besides, it might be good for you t'know there's somebody as has your back."

Carter grunted. His figure, small though it was, momentarily decreased the light entering the cabin as he passed through the doorway and quickly disappeared, moving to his right, toward the south, which was where the larger body of riders seemed to be coming.

Longarm followed, moving left, to the north, where he had heard the lone rider's slow approach.

He carried the heavy shotgun in the crook of his left elbow, his right thumb draped over both hammers, tensed and ready for whatever trouble was to come.

As he moved, he felt the spare shot shells shifting under their own weight inside the waist of his long johns. By the time he had gone a dozen yards, the shells had fallen past his waist and dribbled down his right leg, exiting the bottom. They were lost in the darkness. He knelt and was able to find three of the errant shells. He settled for holding those in his left hand. With the two shells in the shotgun chambers, he had five live rounds to work with.

Those should be more than enough, Longarm figured.

Whoever it was paying Carter a night call would not be expecting much in the way of resistance. Certainly they would not be expecting to face two opponents here.

Longarm moved north about twenty yards, found the bole of a large aspen, and leaned against it, the double-barreled Smith still held casually in the crook of his left arm.

But his eyes and ears were working hard to penetrate the night.

Chapter 13

"This is your warning. The only one you will get." The voice came from Longarm's right, from the direction Carter had taken when he left the cabin. The voice was that of a man. That much was clear, but the sound was muffled, as if the speaker had something—a mask perhaps—draped over his mouth.

"Warning about what?" Carter called back.

The riders seemed to have stopped at the fringe of an aspen grove, Longarm thought. He could hear the jangle of bit chains but could not see the men or their mounts. They were hidden in deep shadow.

"Warning to get out while you can," the voice returned. "You aren't wanted here."

"It's my place," Carter returned, "filed on legal and proper. You have no authority to tell me to leave."

"This is all the authority we need," the voice said, and the darkness was torn apart by three muzzle flashes. All of them, Longarm noticed, were aimed into the sky somewhere above the cabin roof. They were trying to intimidate, not to kill.

More gunshots followed. A dozen or more, one after

another, the night riders taking turns firing pistols into the air.

While all of that noise was going on, the lone rider tried to sneak in under cover of his companions' diversion.

The lone rider was more dangerous than the loud crowd by far, Longarm thought, because unlike the others, this jasper actually wanted to do harm.

He was headed toward the back of the cabin. Intending to set it afire? More than likely, Longarm suspected.

Suspected but did not know with any certainty.

Longarm let the man come on. Let him move past without spotting the waiting deputy marshal. Without spotting that waiting shotgun.

Once the rider was out of the trees into the clearing, the press of his horse's hoofs crunching gravel as he crossed the creek, Longarm slipped in behind him.

He could see the rider silhouetted clearly against a starlit sky.

Longarm pulled the left hammer of his Smith back to full cock and, smiling grimly, let go with a ten-gauge round aimed in thin air a couple feet behind the night rider's head.

"Jesus!" a clear voice shouted.

The horse he was riding began to buck and tear across the clearing in panic, snorting and farting to beat the band, racing belly down into the aspens below the cabin and spooking the horses of the other riders down there so they got into a panic too.

From the little Longarm could see, the rider was clinging to his saddle horn with both hands. Probably instinctively digging in with his spurs too, which was not a response calculated to calm the terrified animal on whose back he was riding.

If it hadn't been so serious, it would have been funny, Longarm thought.

Upon reflection he decided that it *was* funny as hell.

He could hear the frightened horse charging down

through the valley, the other three following behind it until the night was again silent and serene.

Don Carter was suddenly standing in front of him, the former Ranger coming toward him so silently that Longarm had not heard the man's approach, did not realize he was there until he spoke.

"That was you, I take it?"

"Uh-huh," Longarm responded with a chuckle. "Fella came past me bold as brass. Had no idea there could be anybody over this side o' the clearing."

"Did you get him?" Carter asked.

"Didn't try to," Longarm said. "Put a round just behind his hat though. Scared the shit outa him, I bet. His horse too. He was headed toward the back o' your place. No idea what he was gonna do there, as he didn't have a chance to do whatever it woulda been."

"I think I'm happy not to know," Carter said.

"D'you want me to keep watch the rest of the night?" Longarm offered.

"I don't think we need to do that," Carter said. "They won't be back tonight, I think."

"D'you know who they was?" Longarm asked.

"Not exactly. I suspect who might have sent them, but I don't know who those four will have been."

Longarm laughed. "Just look for a bunch with the backs o' their britches smeared thick with the shit we scared out o' them."

"That might give them away indeed," Carter said. "Come along inside now. There is a lot of night left, and we need to get some sleep before daybreak catches us lying abed."

"Mind if I hang on to this sawed-off the rest o' the night? Just in case, like."

"It's yours, Short."

For a moment Longarm was confused. He had forgotten that that was the name he had given himself here. But then, dammit, it was the middle of the night and his sleep had been disrupted by men with guns. He could be forgiven that brief slipup, he hoped.

He followed Carter back inside and felt along the floor to find the pallet he had laid out for his bed.

He was sound asleep again within moments, the double-barreled ten-gauge tucked down by his thigh.

Chapter 14

"Lookee here what I found," Longarm said as he entered the cabin early that next morning. He had gone out to the cathole that served in place of a proper outhouse, and on his way back from taking a shit he stopped to look for the shotgun shells he had dropped the night before when they trickled down through the leg of his long johns. He found the brass shells all right, but he also came up with three pine tar torches, unlit but ready to burn bright and long once a match was touched to them.

"Bastards thought they could burn me out," Carter said. He was standing at the stove frying slices of salt pork and pan bread for their breakfast.

"They were wrong," Longarm said.

"Thanks to you. I owe you for that."

Longarm grunted. "You don't owe me nothing." He grinned. "But I could damn sure use a little o' that stuff in the skillet. It smells so good it's got my saliva running faster'n that creek out there."

"Is that your belly I hear rumbling?" Carter asked, using a long fork to turn the fatty salt pork. "I thought that noise was an avalanche coming down on us. Say, set those torches aside, will you? I can use them in my diggings."

Longarm nodded, stepped outside, and placed the torches against the wall. He returned to the cabin, washed in a bucket beside the stove, and set a pair of tin plates and two tin cups on the rickety table that occupied the center of the room.

"You say you think you know who sent those jaspers last night?"

Carter nodded. "Could be. I'm not sure though." He used an iron hook to pick up the coffeepot from the back of the stove and protected his hand with a rag so he could pour steaming coffee into the two cups Longarm had placed on the table, then he returned the pot to the stove.

He slid the skillet to the front of the stove and picked it up with the hand that had the rag wrapped around it. He carried the skillet to the table and, using the fork, pushed half of the salt pork and pan bread onto each plate.

"Set," he said. "Eat it while it's hot."

"You won't have to ask me twice," Longarm said, straddling one of the stools beside the table and picking up a fork. "Care to tell me what it's all about? Not that it's any of my business. I'm just curious," he said a moment later, around a mouthful of the chewy, grease-covered pan bread.

Carter was busy surrounding his breakfast too. He paused before he answered. "Greed," he said. "What else. The good folk down in Good Hope thought it was something of a joke when I filed a minerals claim up here. Everyone knew there was nothing to find, even though you can pull an assay on a broken brick and find a trace of some sort of mineral. Then I filed a homestead claim on the valley. That aggravated old Kyle Burgen. You won't likely know Burgen, but he is the he-coon around here. Owns half the county and more than half of the town. His livestock used to use the grass up here for summer graze. So the homestead claim pissed him off. All the more so after I brought an ore sample down that showed better than a hundred twenty dollars a ton."

Longarm whistled. "More'n a hundred dollars. That's one helluva payout. What is it? Gold?"

Carter nodded. "Nobody saw it before because everyone looks for quartz as an indicator of gold. This is a vein in common schist."

Longarm smiled. "Whatever the hell that is."

"Plain old stone," Carter told him. "And the truth is, I didn't come up here looking for it. I just wanted a place where I could retire. I intended to have a little garden, maybe some goats for meat and milk. I was digging a root cellar when I found the gold. Now I'm almost sorry that I did. I never figured to be a rich man. Now I worry all the damn time about hanging on to my claim."

Longarm smiled. "Hell, Boss, with any kind of luck that vein will pinch out soon an' you'll be back to not having anything worth stealing. Want some more o' that coffee while I'm up?" He stood and went to the stove, used a rag to get the coffeepot and pour for both of them.

"I almost think that would be lucky," Carter said. "I can go back to being poor but contented with my few dollars a month of pension."

"What are you retired from?" Longarm asked.

"I used to work for the state government back in Texas," Carter said. Which was the truth if not the whole truth. Perhaps, Longarm thought, the folks around Good Hope did not know Don Carter had been a Texas Ranger and could be expected to be a salty old son of a bitch.

"What d'you want me to do today, Boss?" Longarm asked, changing the subject. "What chores need doin'?"

Chapter 15

Longarm emerged from the mouth of the mine adit and
stopped to shake some of the rock dust off his clothes. After
he'd saved the cabin from being burned down, Carter trusted
him enough to allow him to work all that week inside the
mine. Considering how tired he was, Longarm almost
wished Billy's friend was still suspicious of him.

He bent at the waist and beat his clothing until the clouds
of dust coming off his overalls were not quite so dark, then
walked over to the back of the cabin and dipped a double
handful of cold water out of the wash bucket there. He
sluiced off his face, soaked his bandanna and used it to wipe
the back of his neck—Lordy, that cold water did feel
refreshing—and washed his hands with a bit of the soft soap
Carter kept in a broken dish.

Longarm went inside, opened the tin door of the sheepherder stove, and used a stick of fat pine to stir up the coals
from the morning fire. When the pine caught, he added
sticks of split aspen, then larger chunks until he had a good
fire roaring in the little stove.

He carried the coffeepot outside, dumped the cold left-
overs from morning, and filled the pot with fresh water from
the creek. Back inside the cabin, he threw in a couple

handfuls of ground coffee—it seemed quite an extravagance to buy ready-ground coffee instead of raw beans, but then it was Don Carter's money—into the pot and set it on the front of the stove.

Flour, water, lard, and a pinch of salt put the pan bread to fry, but they were out of bacon and nearly out of salt pork. Carter had set some beans on to soak before they headed for the mine that morning, so Longarm dropped in a couple chunks of salt pork and set that on the stove to boil along with the coffee. By the time the little man quit work for the day and returned to the cabin, Longarm felt like he was about to starve after smelling all those good odors.

Carter grabbed a plate and cup, filled both, and sat at the table without a word.

"There's something I ought to tell you," Longarm said as he too brought a full plate and cup and sat down.

Carter grunted an acknowledgment but did not look up from his plate. He looked even more tired than Longarm felt.

"We're 'bout out of meat, Boss. You want me to take a gun and knock down some deer meat tomorrow?"

"No, dammit, I don't like deer meat," Carter said. "Besides, it's too much bother, cleaning and butchering and such. Anyway, we're out of some other things too. The problem is that we can't leave the place empty or some son of a bitch is apt to come along and burn it. Those night riders haven't bothered us for a week, but they could be just waiting to pick their time."

"I can stay and watch the place," Longarm offered.

Carter shook his head. "Better, I think, for you to go down to town. You know the way. I'll give you some money for what we need . . . I'll make up a list tonight." He paused and looked at Longarm. "You can read, can't you? No matter, I suppose. Adamson down at the mercantile can read my scratching even if you can't."

"I can read," Longarm said. The question was not a foolish one. A great many people could not.

"Anyway, I'll make up a list and give you money to pay for it. You can take the wagon down . . ." He peered at Longarm again. "You can drive a team, can't you?"

"Jeez, Boss, quit fretting about what I can or can't do. I can drive a team. Walk an' whistle at the same time without tripping over my own feet too. Now rest easy an' make out your list. I'll take care of it."

Carter nodded and went back to his plate of beans and squaw bread.

Chapter 16

The hides of the two cobs gleamed red in the early morning light. The horses were fractious after being so long without work, so Longarm gave them very little to eat. They were energetic enough without that, but he put a gallon or so of mixed grain into a burlap sack and placed that in the bed of the wagon. He could feed it to the boys once they got to town and had some of the sass worked off.

He gave them a rubdown and cleaned their hooves while they ate, then he stepped back inside the cabin to ask Carter which horse went where.

"Junebug's the wheeler. Put him on the left."

"All right, then which o' the damn things is Junebug?" Longarm asked.

"He's the one with the white up to his hock on the right hind leg. Horace has a scar under his eye." Carter scowled. "They're easy to tell apart. Are you *sure* you can drive a wagon, Short?"

"Yes, dammit, I'm sure." He went back outside and sorted out the unfamiliar harness, then put Junebug on the left and Horace beside him—Carter did seem to choose odd names for his horses, Longarm thought, but then what did he know about it—and hitched them to the ore wagon, which served double duty for whatever function Carter wished. So far he'd had little enough ore to be hauled and no local smelter to haul it to.

Carter came outside about the time Longarm was ready to head down the mountain. "Do you want a gun to carry with you?" the little man offered.

Longarm shook his head. "I'm not going there lookin' for trouble. Might be better if I don't carry one."

"Suit yourself." Carter disappeared into the mine, which was progressing nicely now that there were two of them doing the work. Soon they would have enough high-grade ore stockpiled that they would have to process it by hand or work out some way to get the best pieces to a proper smelter.

Longarm climbed onto the wagon box and took up the lines. "All right, boys. Let's do this thing."

Longarm found Bert Adamson's store without much difficulty. After all, there were not so very many to choose from in Good Hope. He pulled around to the side of the building, only to find the loading dock already occupied, so he stopped on the street, climbed down, and ran a strap from Horace's bit to a nearby hitch rail, then went inside.

Adamson, or whoever the man behind the counter was, looked him over and frowned. "We aren't giving out any charity. Go down to the Methodist church if you want a handout."

Longarm could not blame the man. His clothes had been disreputable to begin with. After the time spent gouging rock out of a mountain, he probably looked like he should be picked up whole and thrown into a rag bag.

"I brought an order from Mr. Carter over on Benton Mountain," Longarm informed the clerk.

"With cash money?"

Longarm nodded. "He sent some money."

"All right then. The boss is busy taking in a load of goods. Do you have the order written out?"

"I do."

"Give it to me then. We'll fill it as soon as we can. An hour, couple hours maybe."

Longarm grunted. There were things he would rather do than wander aimlessly on the streets of Good Hope, Arizona, for the next few hours. He was beginning to wish he had brought some of his own money so he could at least buy himself a drink or three, but he had not thought to do so.

"Ain't hindsight wonderful," he mumbled to himself. More clearly he said, "D'you know Mr. Carter's outfit?"

The clerk nodded. "I do."

"It's tied out front. Just put the stuff in it. I'll come back an' pick it up directly."

"Give me two hours to make sure."

"Fine," Longarm said, although he had no idea what he could do in Good Hope for two hours when he had no money of his own to spend. He headed out the door onto the town's main street.

Chapter 17

Longarm ambled past a saloon, the sharply pleasant scents of pilsner and sawdust reaching him past the batwings, and thought it might be sensible to ask at the post office if there was a letter for him, perhaps, or a telegraph message. After all, Billy knew where he was and might have sent a message for some reason. He found the post office two blocks down and went inside.

There was neither mail nor wire waiting there, a mild disappointment, but Longarm sent Billy Vail a wire—collect—to the boss's home address, with no mention of his office included, letting him know about the night riders. There really was no good news to impart, but he thought Billy should know what was going on down here.

He signed his message just Custis, lest there be any confusion at this end about the Long or the Short of things, and got the wire off by way of a young, skinny, prematurely balding mail clerk. Once the message had been accepted and put in a bin for outgoing traffic, Longarm wandered over to the side of the post office to look over the Wanted posters hanging there. You never knew who you might find among those fliers. Maybe a friend.

He was reading the Arizona Wants when he heard a female voice at the counter.

"Good morning, Johnny."

"G'morning, Miz Pride. You have, um, you have something here today. It's a package. Let me get it for you."

"Thank you, Johnny."

The lady's voice sounded vaguely familiar, and Longarm turned to see. Pride? Good Lord. Eleanor Pride.

The lady saw and recognized Longarm about the same time he did the same with her. Her eyes went wide and she said, "Custis! What are you doing here?"

He quickly laid a finger over his lips to shush Ellie before she might blurt out his name or mention anything about him being a lawman. Then just as quickly he smiled and stepped over to her. "It's good to see you again, Ellie. How are you? How is George? What are you doing here?"

Ellie's smile changed to a frown and she said, "You haven't heard then."

"Heard what?"

"George passed away last spring. The doctor said it was his heart."

"Good Lord, Ellie. He always seemed so strong and . . ."

She nodded. He thought the memories were bringing her close to tears, even though she would have long since adjusted to the fact of her husband's death.

Eleanor Hamilton had been one of Longarm's ladyfriends at one time. Their relationship had not been serious. Then Longarm introduced Ellie to his drinking buddy George Pride. George had been smitten with an intense love at first sight. He had the decency to ask Longarm's permission to court the pretty lady, then moved in and swept Ellie off her feet. They were married within a matter of months.

That had been . . . Longarm had to think back for a moment . . . three years? Four? A long time anyway.

"I'm sorry, Ellie. Truly sorry to hear that."

Johnny the clerk came back to the window with a rather

large pasteboard box covered in brown wrapping paper and tied with string. "Here you go, Miz Pride." He pushed the box forward.

"Let me carry that for you, Ellie," Longarm said, stepping forward to take the box from the clerk.

"Do I need to sign for it, Johnny?"

"No, ma'am, you don't."

"Thank you then. And thank you, Custis."

"You lead to wherever this needs to go, Ellie. I'll follow."

"It isn't far. I have a little shop three blocks over. I'll show you."

Longarm tucked the box under his arm and walked along beside Eleanor to a storefront with a small sign in the window saying DRESSMAKER.

"Dressmaker?" Longarm asked while Ellie was unlocking the door.

"A girl has to make a living somehow," she said. She pulled the door open and ushered him in before her. "I get a little business for my dresses." She laughed. "I'm better at it than you might have suspected. Better than I suspected myself, to tell the truth. Now I'm going to try making ladies' hats too. In that box you are carrying are feathers, facings, that sort of thing. And, I hope, some hatters' felt blanks."

"Blanks?" he asked.

"The little caps the hats are built on," she explained.

"Oh," he said sagely, just like he understood whatever the hell it was Ellie had said.

"You can set it over there."

Longarm placed the box where she indicated while Ellie carefully locked the door behind them. "When do you open?" he asked.

"Not until we've had a chance to catch up on things. The shop can wait. How long has it been, Custis? Four years?"

"Something like that. But while I think about it, I'm not using my proper name here. Down here I'm known as Custis Short."

"Oh, my. I'll certainly remember that," Ellie said. "I wouldn't want to say anything that could put you in danger."

"It ain't anything like that. It'd just be annoying, not dangerous. But I'd appreciate you keepin' my right name to yourself for the time being."

Ellie stepped close to him, disregarding his ragged appearance, and said, "Kiss me, Custis."

He leaned down and gave her a light peck on the forehead.

"Not like that, dammit," she said. Then her mouth was covering his and her tongue was pressed into his mouth.

"You taste good," he said moments later.

"Shut up." She came to him again, grinding her hips against his and reaching down to grope his crotch. "How do you get this thing off, anyway?" She was feeling for a fly, but there was none on his bib overalls.

"Let me show you," he offered and quickly unfastened the large brass buttons that held the denim suspenders to the bib of the overalls.

His overalls dropped away, and Ellie unbuttoned the front of his long johns. She reached inside for his rapidly stiffening cock and pulled it out.

"Oh, my," she breathed. "I remember this so well. Do you mind?"

"Not hardly," he told her. It was a completely honest statement too.

Ellie dropped to her knees at his feet and pressed his dick, hot and hard now, against her cheek. "I remember how good your cum tastes. It has a flavor that is almost sweet. George was a dear man, but his cum was bitter. I didn't mind doing him, but it never tasted good. Yours I could drink by the glassful."

"Ellie, darlin', that's more'n I really want to know."

"Of course. Sorry." She petted his shaft like you would pet a cat, then reached between his legs and tickled his balls for a moment, before taking the head of his cock into her mouth. She pulled his foreskin back and swirled her tongue around the head.

"Lovely," she said a moment later when she released him, the air on his prick cold where she had left it wet.

Longarm stroked her hair and the back of her head, and Ellie went back to sucking him. She kept that up for a minute or so, then looked up and said, "I live in the back of the shop, dear. I have a bed there."

Longarm hooked a finger under her chin and then lifted her, guiding Ellie to her feet. He pulled his overalls up off the floor so he did not trip over them, then followed her to the back of her shop.

He kicked out of his boots and stepped out of the overalls while Ellie was unbuttoning her dress and getting out of it.

Ellie Pride had put on some weight since they were lovers those years ago, but she was still a handsome figure of a woman. Her tits were heavier now and drooped somewhat, her nipples larger and darker than he remembered. She had a thick patch of dark, curly pubic hair set between thighs that were rather heavy now. He remembered her as having had very slender legs before, and there was a little gray showing at her temples.

Not that it mattered. Not that any of that mattered worth a damn when sweet Ellie came to him and once again dropped to her knees before him.

By way of tugs and pulls and gentle pushes, Ellie moved Longarm to her bed and onto the down-filled mattress. During that process she never once allowed his cock to leave the warm heat of her mouth. She pressed him down onto his back and crawled on top of him so that her belly was pressed hard against his chin and her legs straddled his head.

She smelled of soap and perfume and some sweet, soft essence of woman. She was clean and she tasted as good as she smelled.

Ellie took him into her mouth deep then, taking nearly all of his shaft into herself. He could feel the head of his cock strike hard against the ring of cartilage at the beginning of her throat. She pushed, gagged just a little, and then his dick slid through that slight obstruction and fully into her throat. The feel of it was so fine that Longarm was close to coming then and there, but he managed to hold back, and Ellie soon was bobbing up and down on him, his cock slipping from throat to mouth and back again, time after time, while Ellie fondled his balls and tickled his asshole with a fingernail.

She wriggled her hips to remind him that he was not alone on the bed, and he dipped his beak into the wet folds of her pussy.

Ellie tasted every bit as good as she smelled. The flavor of her juices was delicate and very pleasant. He ran his tongue into her hole briefly, then pulled back just a little and began to lick the tiny button of pleasure that hid at the top— or bottom from the upside-down direction he now found her in as she lay on top of him—of her slit. He remembered that was what she particularly enjoyed, and that had not changed in the slightest. As soon as his tongue began to lick and titillate her clitoris, Ellie's hips began to writhe and her breath came quicker and quicker, until she was panting and bucking up and down against his probing, sucking mouth.

She came almost at once. And then again, the second time crying out loud.

Longarm stopped holding back and let his own climax come, his juices spurting deep into Ellie's throat.

She clutched hard at his cock, like she could not get enough of it, and she sucked until the last drop of his jism had been taken and swallowed.

Longarm smiled. "A gentleman always appreciates a lady that swallows," he said.

Ellie's response was to wriggle her hips so that her pussy wiped back and forth across his lips. Then she laughed. "Damn, it's good to see you again, Custis," she said.

"That feelin' is mutual, ma'am," he assured her. "Now git up off me."

"You aren't done yet, are you?" she asked.

"No, but I want t'swap ends so's I can plant my pole where it rightly belongs. Not," he added, "that there's anything wrong with that sweet mouth o' yours. But I'm hankerin' for a fuck t'go with that other most excellent activity."

"Then a fuck you shall have, sir," Ellie told him. "A fuck and then a drink, how does that sound?"

Longarm grinned. "I knew there was some reason I like you, girl. You just surely do know how t'please a gentleman."

Ellie chuckled. And reached for his cock.

Chapter 18

Longarm lay back, head propped on two of Ellie's pillows, while she fixed a pot of fresh coffee. That was not exactly the sort of drink he had in mind, but coffee would certainly do. Once the pot was boiling, she came back to bed.

"Damn, woman, I think you look better nekkid than most ladies do with their clothes on," he said. That was a fib but only a little one. There had been a time when he might have meant what he said quite literally, but that had been a few years ago.

"You can't fool me, Custis. You think that of every woman you see." Ellie laughed and flicked her tongue over his left nipple.

He reached for her, thinking to have a little more of that sweet essence, but she placed a hand against his chest to hold him just a little way off.

"You have to get up and get dressed now, cowboy. You might be able to laze around all day doing nothing, but I have to work. I need to get dressed and open my shop." She smiled to take the sting out of the rejection. "A girl has to make a living, you know, and as much as I like to fuck, I don't want to have to do it with any smelly stranger who comes along and puts a coin in my hand. I have to either make a living with this shop or become one of those ladies of the night."

Longarm grunted and sat up on the side of the bed. He reached for his clothes and began pulling them on. "Remember, will ya please, that my name is Short an' I'm just drifting through. I ain't no deputy U.S. marshal. Leastways not so far as anybody around here knows."

"I'll remember," Ellie promised. "Come along into the shop with me, Custis. We can have our coffee there," she said as she finished dressing.

The coffee was good and the company even better, but after forty-five minutes or so customers began showing up in Ellie's place of business and Longarm excused himself from the flutter and gossip of Good Hope's ladies. He had the impression that Ellie Pride and her dressmaking shop had become the female equivalent of a saloon, except in this case it was a place where women could come to relax and let their hair down, figuratively speaking that is. He certainly did not want to intrude on that sort of conversation so he gave Ellie a chaste peck on the forehead and a promise that he would see her again while he was in the vicinity of Good Hope.

He let himself out onto the street and began walking back toward Bert Adamson's store, where by now the goods Don Carter ordered should be loaded into the wagon and ready to head back up the mountain.

He was about halfway there and was just approaching one of the town's few saloons when a short, dark, handsomely tailored gentleman stepped in front of him. The gent wore a diamond tie pin that if real would surely cost a year's salary for an average working man. His vest and spats were in a matching pattern of yellow and brown, and he carried a cane with a crystal head in the shape of an eagle's beak. A delicate scent of bay rum or some similar tonic rose off of him.

"Excuse me, but do you have a moment?" the impeccably groomed little man said.

"I reckon," Longarm told him, "but I ain't lookin' for work if that's what you have in mind. I already got a job."

The fellow smiled. "Not what I intend. I would, however, like to offer you a drink."

"Me? Why?"

"You are Short, are you not?"

Longarm grinned and from his six-foot-plus height looked down at the crown of the little man's head. "We aren't gonna start crackin' wise about how tall one or t'other of us is, are we?"

"What? What do you mean by that?"

"Oh, nothin'. What was you saying about a drink?"

"You are Short, aren't you? The gentleman who is, um, employed by Donald Carter?"

"I confess," Longarm told him. "That's me."

"Then may I offer you a drink, Mr. Short?"

"Now, it ain't really often you'd catch me turnin' down a drink, though I got t'warn you, I got no money to reciprocate the offer."

"Nor is any necessary. Please. Come inside here and lift a glass with me. There is, um, something I would like to discuss with you."

Longarm shrugged. "Sure. Sounds all right to me. But I didn't catch your name, mister."

"I am Kyle Burgen, Mr. Short. You may have heard the name."

Longarm looked off into the distance, feigning deep thought. Then he shook his head and lied, "No, sir, I don't reckon that I have."

"No matter," Burgen said airily. But that too was a lie. Longarm could see that the little man expected his name to be known—and feared—anywhere around the town of Good Hope. "Come inside. We will have that drink. And talk." He even pushed the batwings aside and held them open for Longarm to precede him into the saloon.

Chapter 19

Longarm settled down with a bottle of truly excellent rye whiskey—Maryland distilled, of course—and a pitcher of fresh lager on the table. Burgen had a glass in front of him, but he did not bother to pour anything into it. Longarm decided this might be a meeting that required a clear head, so he went light on both the rye and the beer.

"What is it you're wantin', Mr. Burgen?" he asked once a shot of the rye and half a glass of beer were gone. Burgen helpfully reached across the table and refilled Longarm's whiskey glass.

"Would you like a smoke, Mr. Short? Or don't you indulge?"

"Oh, I indulge the hell outa cheroots when I can pay for 'em." He smiled and added, "Which doesn't happen t'be now."

"Cheroots, you say?"

"Yes, sir."

Burgen immediately got up, went to the bar, and had the apron bring out a cedarwood box from beneath the counter. When Burgen returned, he handed Longarm half a dozen excellent, pale-leaf cheroots and a block of matches to go with them.

"Now, you are one fine gentleman," Longarm said, biting the twist off one of the cheroots, licking the shaft, and striking a match to it. Lordy, but after going so long without a smoke, that one tasted better than merely fine.

"You are entirely welcome, Mr. Short. In fact I've instructed Addison there to give you drinks and cigars anytime you wish. On me, of course."

"Mr. Burgen, I am not the savviest man you've ever knowed, but even I can figure out that there's something you need me to do. It'd please me if you'd come right out an' say what it is."

Burgen tipped his chair back and seemed to contemplate what his answer would be—if any. After a few seconds he let the chair ease back onto its legs. He glanced around to make sure there was no one close enough to overhear.

"Do, Mr. Short? I do not want you to *do* anything. In fact I explicitly want you to *not* do."

Longarm swallowed back his rye, had a little of the beer chaser, and poured himself some more of the whiskey. Damn, but that was good rye. He made a mental note to remember that label. Surely someone in Denver could come up with some of it for him. "So what is it that I ain't supposed to do, Mr. Burgen?"

"Should anyone come calling at the Carter mine some night, it would be a good thing if your shotgun misfired, Mr. Short. You needn't shoot at all." Burgen cleared his throat and looked away, then said, "You might receive a rather handsome gratuity if you were to do that."

Longarm grinned. "How handsome are we talkin' here?"

"Let's just say it would be more than a man's monthly salary."

"Mr. Burgen, you are a kind and generous soul," Longarm said over the rim of the whiskey glass.

"Do we understand each other, Mr. Short?"

"Perfectly, Mr. Burgen."

The businessman pushed his chair back and stood. He nodded to the barkeep and to Longarm said, "Keep that bottle, Mr. Short. Consider it a down payment." Then he turned and headed for the batwings at a crisp pace.

Chapter 20

That was interesting, Longarm thought. Not that there had been very much doubt to begin with about who was behind the attacks on Don Carter's mine. But it was nice to have Burgen himself confirm the suspicions.

Longarm tossed off the rest of the whiskey in his glass and jammed the cork firmly into the mouth of the bottle, then stood, leaving the rest of his beer on the table. He did pick up the rye, though. No way was he going to leave that behind for the bartender to sell a second time. Burgen had paid for it. Fine. The sorry son of a bitch might consider it a bribe. Longarm grinned to himself. Wasn't he going to be disappointed when that plan did not take.

Longarm waved the bottle to show the bartender— Addison, had Burgen called him?—that he was taking it, then he too headed for the batwings.

He was about two paces short of the exit when Maxwell Jeffords walked in.

Longarm sighed. He knew about three people in Good Hope, Arizona, and two of them, this big SOB Jeffords and town marshal Stonecipher, were trouble, although in different ways.

"You!" Jeffords said, making the lone word sound like an accusation.

"Me," Longarm agreed.

"I'm gonna pound your ass," Jeffords said.

"No," Longarm said, "you are not. You don't have your pals to back you up this time, you big pile o' shit."

The big brawler reared back for a haymaker, and Longarm bashed him over the head with the whiskey bottle that happened to be in his hand.

The bottle broke, sending a cascade of good rye whiskey over Jeffords's face and into his beard.

"Damn you," Longarm complained, "that was awful good whiskey you just wasted."

Jeffords wiped the fiery liquor out of his eyes and shook his head to clear it of the cobwebs that were suddenly there.

Then he lowered his head and charged.

Longarm tossed the broken bottle aside and sidestepped the bull rush. He was only partially clear when the top of Jeffords's skull, blood and whiskey and all, crashed into his ribs on his right side. Longarm pounded the back of Jeffords's head with a closed fist, driving the big man to his knees.

Jeffords grabbed at Longarm's legs and succeeded in grasping his right leg. He tried to pull Longarm down to the saloon floor and did manage to unbalance the tall deputy.

Longarm jammed his foot back onto the planks, lifted his other foot, and stomped on the back of Jeffords's wrist.

"You son of a bitch!" Jeffords bellowed.

Longarm stomped him again, getting him on the forearm this time.

Jeffords let go of Longarm's leg and rolled away, scrambled crablike to the side, and came back onto his feet, once more charging at Longarm with his head lowered.

Longarm stepped back, gauged speed and distance, and delivered a right to the side of Jeffords's jaw with just about all the power he could muster. If that did not do the job,

Longarm thought, then he was in deep shit, because this was one big, strong bastard.

Fortunately the punch connected solidly and had the desired effect. Jeffords folded, out cold. He hit the sawdust facedown and did not even bounce.

Longarm walked over to the bar. He was breathing hard and the knuckles on his right hand were scraped and bloody, but at least he was the one who was standing on his own hind legs.

"Sorry 'bout that," he said to Addison the bartender. "I hope you ain't gonna call Marshal Stonecipher for I'd surely hate to have to spend another night in his hotel."

"I don't expect to," Addison said. "I saw the way it happened." He shrugged. "Max does that sort of thing, you know."

Longarm grinned. "I'm beginnin' to find out."

"You want another bottle to replace that one?" Addison offered. "On Mr. Burgen. He said you should have whatever you want."

"Sure." The grin flashed again. "But put it on Max's tab."

Addison laughed and turned to fetch the bottle.

Jeffords was beginning to stir when Longarm stepped over him and headed up the street to collect Don Carter's wagonload of supplies.

Chapter 21

"It took you long enough," Carter complained when Longarm carried the first load of supplies inside the cabin and began stowing them where they belonged.

"Yeah, well, I'm glad to see you too."

"Did you have any trouble?" Carter asked.

"Nothin' I couldn't handle." He smiled. "You'll be happy to know me and Mr. Burgen got acquainted."

Carter stopped what he was doing, which was drinking a cup of coffee, and raised an eyebrow.

Longarm chuckled. "He offered me a bribe."

"He offered . . ."

"Which o' course confirms what you already knowed about him bein' the source o' those thugs that come by offerin' to provide you with a bonfire."

"I suppose it does. What did you tell him?"

"Didn't tell him much of anything. Gave him the impression, though, that I can be bought."

"Can you?" Carter asked.

"Blunt son of a bitch, ain't you?"

"Yes, I am. Can you?"

"Can I be bought?" Longarm shrugged. "Tell you the

truth, I don't rightly know. What I do know is that I've never yet encountered the man with enough money to do the job."

"That includes Kyle Burgen?"

Longarm nodded. "That includes Burgen. By the bye, whilst he was tryin' to bribe me, he made it pretty clear there is gonna be another raid out here."

"Did he say when this might be?"

"No. Now, if you'll quit jawing at me, I'll go fetch in the rest o' your shit. Those boys been in harness a long time. They're due for a feed an' a roll in the dirt."

"Let me help you with the rest of those things."

"I'll be damned. The boss is actually gonna do something around here for a change," Longarm said.

Carter gave him a dirty look. But then both of them knew that the little man drove himself like a rented mule from sunup to sundown day after day.

Longarm went back out to the wagon, Carter close on his heels. Between them they made short work of the unloading, then Longarm led the team over to the fenced trap to unhitch the big horses and bed them down for the night.

While he was out there, he gave some thought to the mine and the cabin and the way Carter's holdings were situated at the head of the high valley.

Burgen's raiders would almost certainly come at them from down below in the valley. They could not come in from above or they would be fumbling around on loose shale. That would be the next thing to suicidal in the dark, even if they left their horses somewhere and came down on foot. Certainly such an approach would send a cascade of loose scree down ahead of them. Loose and noisy.

It was possible, if barely, that they might try to come in from one side or the other. Still, the most likely approach, Longarm decided, would be right up the valley.

And that, once they broke out of the trees, could be easily defended against.

"If you don't mind," he said when supper was over and the dishes done, "I'm gonna move out tonight."

Carter paused, then nodded. "I can't blame you, Short. This isn't your fight. Thank you for doing everything that you have." The little man stood and went to the wood box. He dug around inside it and came up with a small leather pouch. He pulled the string to open it, spilled a scant handful of coins into the palm of his hand, selected a five-dollar half eagle, and held it out to Longarm.

"What's this for?"

"Pay. I know you said you would work for found, but you've earned this."

"Now, looka here. First off, I don't want no pay. You don't owe me shit. Secondly, I ain't goin' nowhere. When I said I'd be moving out, I didn't mean that I'll be moving on. I won't run out on a man in the middle of his troubles. I'll stick right here till this is worked out.

"What I meant is that I'm gonna move outa this cabin. The four walls cramp me. I like to be able to move around. Besides, I can hear better outside. I'll bed down somewhere down in those trees. Not too close to the creek as I wanta be able to hear if anybody is moving up the valley. An' this time I'm thinking they won't come with torches. They won't want to be seen so easy. This time they'll come dark an' quiet. With guns instead o' those pine knot torches. This time I'm betting they'll come to kill, not to burn."

"I agree," Carter said. "You have good instincts for this sort of thing, Short." He fingered his beard and added, "Have you ever done any time as a lawman?"

"Now that you put it to me direct . . . yes. I have."

"In Texas?"

Longarm shook his head. "No, sir. Not exactly."

"Ever been on the other side of the law?"

Longarm grinned. "Now you're gettin' personal."

"Sorry. That isn't the sort of question you ask a man. I apologize."

"Apology accepted." Longarm picked up his carpetbag, opened it, and brought out his Peacemaker. "I notice you don't look surprised," he said as he belted it on. Damn but he felt better once he had that Colt back where it belonged.

"I'm not," Carter said. "I looked in there while you were down in town today."

"Turnabout is fair play an' all that," Longarm responded. "I've looked into pretty much every nook an' cranny o' this place while you was in the mine too."

"Did you find my pouch?"

"I did," Longarm said with a nod.

"You didn't take anything."

"Wasn't mine to take."

Carter grunted. "Will you want the shotgun or a rifle to sleep with?"

"One of each, I reckon. And a blanket if I can have the loan of one."

"Take anything you think you might need, but I should know where you intend to be. I wouldn't want to shoot you by mistake."

"If they get past me, I won't be in any shape to worry about that, so go ahead an' shoot whatever comes nigh. If I come in at all, it won't be till morning," Longarm said, heading for the trunk where Carter kept his guns, "but for what it's worth, I expect to set up somewhere down below the horse trap so's I can hear 'em come up the valley."

Chapter 22

They came on the fifth night, in the dark of the moon. It was certainly no accident that they waited until they had a moonless night, Longarm figured. They came in the dead dark, sometime past midnight, he judged, and they came as quiet as they could. Which was not particularly quiet.

A small herd of elk or cattle would have made the same amount of noise. Until they decided to put on a sneak. Then, Longarm knew, an elk could make like a ghost, a will-o'-the-wisp, day or night. He had hunted elk, on stands much like this one, and knew an animal passed below him without his ever seeing or hearing it.

Not so with these fellows.

Four of them again, he judged. He wondered if they were the same four. And what their instructions were.

It is one thing to hoorah a man or to haze him out of town. It is something else entirely to commit cold-blooded, deliberate murder. What these men seemed to have in mind was, in fact, murder.

One thing was sure. If Kyle Burgen intended to move Don Carter off this land, the only way he could accomplish it would be to kill the retired Ranger.

It was Longarm's intention to make sure no harm came

to Billy's friend, whatever the desires of these men trying—
without a whole hell of a lot of success—to sneak up on
Carter in the night.

They were perhaps a hundred yards below Longarm
when they reached the aspen. They dismounted there and
began their sneak.

Longarm was seated with his back to them, facing
up-valley with his back against the bole of a huge old aspen
tree, blanket wrapped around his shoulders. A fully loaded
Winchester .44-40 was propped against the tree by his left
shoulder. One of the ten-gauge L.C. Smiths lay across
his lap.

Longarm listened to the men's slow and cautious approach
until they were within forty yards or so. Then he slipped the
blanket off his shoulders and let it fall to the ground. He
stood and turned around, leaning against the stout aspen so
the tree was between himself and Burgen's gunmen.

When the raiders were within twenty yards or so, he
draped a thumb over the hammers of the Smith and eared
them back to full cock. The shotgun was loaded with single-
aught buckshot. Just the ticket for thin-skinned game like
mule deer. Or men. A load of buck can cut a man down like
a scythe through wheat, and at close quarters or in darkness
there is nothing better.

Habit made him transfer the Smith to his left hand for a
moment. With his right he reached down to touch the butt
of his Colt—just satisfying himself that the revolver was
where it ought to be, its position and angle in the holster
exactly the way he liked it.

It was. He took the Smith in both hands again.

Longarm was calm. But it might also have been true that
his heartbeat quickened just a little.

This was no game he was playing, and the quarry out
there would be shooting back as soon as he opened the ball.

He licked dry lips. And waited.

Chapter 23

He had fretted about this. Now the moment had arrived, and he just could not force himself to do what common sense told him that he should. Plain, ordinary sense told him he should wait until he had the opportunity, then open up on these men with both barrels.

With any sort of luck he would put one on the ground immediately. Perhaps more. At least he might wound a couple, and that would send the whole pack running for home with their tails between their legs.

He should shoot without warning. That was when he would have the best chance for success.

But . . . dammit . . . years of representing the law simply would not allow him to shoot first.

He knew that he should. He could not do it.

He took a deep breath.

"United States deputy marshal," he shouted into the night. "Stop where you are."

The answer was predictable.

Three sheets of yellow fire blossomed in the trees ten or eleven yards below Longarm's chosen stand. Three gunshots, then quickly a fourth.

Longarm had no idea where any of the bullets went.

Certainly none came near him, and he did not think any hit the tree he was standing behind either.

He leveled the Smith at the first gun flare he saw and squeezed the front trigger, then fought down the recoil and moved his finger to the back trigger. He blinked, trying to recover his night vision and his hearing after the huge flare of fire practically under his nose and the crash of the heavy ten-gauge shot, then shifted his aim just a little toward where he thought another of the lances of fire had been and squeezed again.

He heard someone scream.

Another was moaning, thrashing around in the brush those few yards downslope.

"Jimmy. Jesus, Jimmy, help me."

"Quiet, damn you, or I'll finish you off my own self."

"Help me, Jimmy."

Longarm dropped the Smith and snatched up the Winchester. He pointed from the hip rather than bother trying to aim at something he could not see. Pointed and fired. Then he cranked the lever and fired again and again, as fast as he could seat a fresh cartridge and pull the trigger.

The sounds of gunfire hammered the dark, and the muzzle flashes completely destroyed any night vision he might have had remaining, but down below him he could hear the crash of men charging heedlessly through the aspen grove, running as hard and as fast as they could go.

None of them bothered trying to return Longarm's fire. These men were amateurs, he thought. No hardass hired gunmen among them. Likely they were town drunks or layabouts that Kyle Burgen had promised an easy payday.

Longarm grunted. He knelt and found the Smith lying in the leaf litter on the forest floor.

He replaced the Winchester against the sturdy aspen, broke open the action of the Smith, plucked the spent brass shotgun shells out of the twin breeches, dropped those on the ground, and reloaded with fresh shells from his pocket.

He remained standing for a time, listening, until both sight and hearing returned to normal. Then he turned around to face uphill toward the cabin and once more sat with his back to the tree and the blanket wrapped around his shoulders.

He sat that way, teeth chattering from the high country chill, until daybreak. Then he again stood, his knees crackling, and yawned and stretched.

He walked down through the trees to where he was sure the raiders had been when he fired at them. There were no bodies on the ground there, but he did find several blood pools and some spatter. He had hit someone; he had no idea who or how bad. The amount of blood at one spot suggested at least one of the raiders might have died, but Longarm could not know that. Not for sure. Not that it would worry him if he'd killed one or more of the bastards. They had come up here, four of them, wanting to commit murder or at least mayhem.

Custis Long had no sympathy for any of the sons of bitches. No sympathy and scant curiosity. He had done what needed doing and that was that.

He went back uphill, picked up the Winchester, and, stomach rumbling, walked stiffly up to the cabin, where he sure as hell hoped Don Carter had flapjacks and side meat cooking by now.

Chapter 24

It turned out to be biscuits instead of pancakes, but the side meat was there and so was coffee, hot and black and very welcome on a cold, high country morning.

"Well?" Carter asked when Longarm came up to the cabin.

"I found plenty o' blood, but they carried off whoever it was as got hit. At least the one, maybe two o' them. I ain't for sure. Couldn't see a damn thing on a dark night in that timber, especially after I fired that first one. The muzzle flash had me blinkin' until I got tears in my eyes, but they was in just as bad a shape."

"I stood ready up here, but of course none of them got this far. You did a good job, Short."

"Good enough to deserve a cup o' that coffee I'm smelling?"

Carter laughed and grabbed a tin cup off the shelf. He even poured the coffee for Longarm and set it on the table. "Sit. I'll have our breakfast ready in a minute."

Longarm sighed. "Bastard has declared open warfare now, Boss. So what d'you figure to do next?"

"I've done nothing wrong and I'm not going anywhere," Carter said. "That said, we have about a wagonload of high-

grade ore ready to ship. I suppose I need to figure out what
to do with the stuff now that I have it."

Longarm smiled. "Don't expect much in the way of sympathy for your problem of how to dispose of all that gold."

"I suppose that would be a lot to ask for, wouldn't it?"
Carter said with a chuckle.

"You have to leave the place deserted while you take the
load down to wherever it's goin'. Could be there won't be
anything to come back to. They could come up here an' burn
it down while there's nobody to defend it."

"If the cabin is gone, no matter. If it comes to that, I can
rebuild. The land will still be here."

"An' the mine," Longarm put in.

"Yes. It would be hard to steal a hole in the ground."

"Unless you go about it the way Burgen wants to. Either
kill you or . . . What would be his next step?"

"Legal challenges to my ownership, but he has already
tried that. I filed papers with the county and, more importantly, with the territorial government. My claim is rock-
solid. Which he has already learned. That is why he is
trying force now. First guile. Now gunfire." Carter opened
the stove and pulled out a pan of biscuits, then set them onto
the table where Longarm could reach them. He took the
skillet off the top of the stove and speared the slabs of fatback one by one. The first four he put onto Longarm's plate.
The rest he gave to himself.

"Dig in," he said. "You earned it last night."

"I'll go out again tonight if you don't mind," Longarm
said. "I doubt they'll come back again any time soon, but
it's always better to be prepared."

"But you aren't getting any sleep, sitting out there night
after night," Carter protested. "I can take some turns at that."

"No," Longarm said, "you're workin' the mine all day
every day. Way it is now, I can rest up during the day an' sit
out there at night. Anyway, I doze while I'm out there. It
ain't like I'm going completely without sleep."

"Whatever you think best," Carter said. He returned to the table and sat, reaching for a biscuit, breaking it apart, and laying a chunk of side meat between the two halves to make a sandwich of sorts. After a moment he looked up and peered across the table at the man he thought was a drifter and something of a bum. He mused aloud, "I don't even know you, Short, yet somehow I find myself putting my life in your hands with those marauders. That isn't like me. Not usually. What is it about you . . .?"

Longarm laughed. "It's because I work so cheap, that's what." He picked up a slab of the fatback and took a bite. The salted pork, fried crisp, was a pleasure. "You're a good cook, Boss. If you had a pussy, I think I'd propose marriage to ya."

"Try that, mister, and you'll be the next one gunned down around here," Carter said.

Longarm laughed again and reached for the biscuits.

Chapter 25

"If you don't mind," Carter said two days later, "I'll go down and see if I can scare up a buyer for this load of ore."

"Any idea what it's worth?" Longarm asked.

Carter shook his head. "No idea at all. Gold isn't something I've ever really paid attention to in the past. I only wanted this property because of the isolation . . . I wanted to be well away from people for a while . . . and because it has some decent grass on it. I only wanted to run a few head of horses up here and be able to live a quiet life by myself." He shrugged. "Then I found the gold. To tell you the truth, Short, I'm almost sorry that I did. Life would have been simpler had I stuck to my original plan."

"You could always forget the gold and shut the mine," Longarm suggested.

"I might have done that except after I found the gold and started digging it out of the ground, I went down to town to buy picks, shovels, things like that, and I opened my fool mouth about my good luck up here. That was all it took. Kyle Burgen decided he should be the one to benefit from my find. He set about trying to gain possession legally. Now illegally. The man just doesn't know when to back off and accept defeat."

Longarm smiled. "Seems as how you don't neither."

"No, I suppose you're right," Carter admitted. "Anyway, I want to leave you up here to watch the place while I go down and see what I can learn about how to dispose of this stuff now that we have it."

"If you don't mind riding down there on one of those wide-ass dray horses, I'll start loading the wagon while you're away. I reckon it's about time for that."

"Yes, indeed," Carter said.

Longarm put the big horses in harness and hitched them to the freight wagon. He drove it up close to the mouth of the gold mine and set the brake, then took the horses back down to the trap. He stripped the harness from both animals and draped it over the fence. Not that it needed to dry in the thin mountain air. The horses had not been used anywhere near heavily enough for them to break a sweat.

He left the bit and bridle on one of the animals and led it up to the cabin, where Don Carter had washed and was changing into a suit and tie.

Longarm poked his head inside, still holding onto the reins of the dray horse, and asked, "Say, Boss, d'you have a saddle around here anyplace?"

"No, and if I did, it surely wouldn't fit anything that broad. No reason I can't ride bareback. It isn't all that far down to town."

"I have him ready for you."

"I'll be out in a minute."

Carter was as good as his word. He came out dressed in his town best and said, "Give me a leg up, will you. I could get up on him by myself, but it would take a half hour and I'd be worn out by the time I made it."

Longarm held his hands cupped together, took Carter's bent knee in them, and lifted the little man onto the cob's back. Longarm handed the reins up to him, and Carter took a moment to coil them and sort them into his hands. The workhorse accepted the presence of the man on its back, but it never would make a saddle horse and still had to be plow-reined.

"Are you gonna be all right?"

"Sure. You just take care of things here. I'll be back this afternoon."

"Whatever you say, Boss."

"Is there anything I can get for you while I'm in town?" Carter offered.

"A bottle an' maybe some cigars. Anything cheap will do. Rum crooks or whatever. I'm just perishin' for a smoke, that's all."

"I'll see what I can find," Carter said. He thumped the big sorrel with his heels, shook the lines, and got the horse into motion. Longarm watched him into the trees, then turned and walked up to the mine to begin loading the wagon with the best of the ore Carter had collected.

Chapter 26

Longarm removed his heavy, canvas gloves and placed them on the floor of the driving box, then walked down to the cabin for a drink of leftover coffee—cold and stout and nasty but better than nothing—and sat down to take a break. The wagon was fully loaded now, although there was still some high-grade ore remaining for another trip, veins of nearly pure gold filtering through like spider tracks.

What Longarm wanted most now was a cigar. He had none and was even out of the cheap tobacco he had brought with him. He was beginning to wish he hadn't hidden his association with Billy Vail. At least if Carter knew him to be a deputy marshal he could spend freely instead of pretending to be a drifting bum.

Of course if he had announced himself, Carter would have closed the door on him, and there was no way Billy's friend could work his mine and defend it by himself as well. And unlike Burgen, Don Carter did not have the means to hire a gang of thugs. Not even with this mine, which could play out and become worthless at the next swing of a pick.

That was the thing with gold mines, especially the mines—like Carter's—that showed strings of nearly pure gold lacing through the rock. They were aberrations and could pinch out at any moment. Longarm had lived in Colorado and been around the mining activity there long enough to know that much about it.

He took a swallow of the bitter coffee, made a sour face, and poured the rest of the cup back into the pot. He opened the firebox on the little sheepherder's stove and poked around in the ashes with a splinter of fat pine. He could not find a live coal and mumbled a few curses. Surely he had not been up there working all that long. But apparently he had.

He really had not noticed the passage of time. But then he had been busy. Time only drags when you do, he thought.

He grabbed the small, flat-bladed shovel that lay on the floor beneath the stove and pulled the ashes, dumping them into a metal bucket that also was kept close to hand. Once the firebox had been cleared, he laid a new fire, starting with more pine splinters and building a pyramid with larger pieces of the pine, then putting on some split aspen and, finally, some good-sized chunks of aspen.

He struck a match to his fire, made sure it was burning properly, and closed the firebox door.

He set the coffeepot back onto the top of the stove and pulled it to the front, where it would receive the most heat from the flames underneath it. Then he adjusted the flue to baby the new fire along.

No wonder he was tired now, he thought, if it was so late in the day.

Longarm walked outside and tried to gauge where the sun might be, but it had long since disappeared behind the mountain that lay to the west of Don Carter's property. Its position was impossible to determine, and the nearby aspen grove was too dense to give a good look at shadows. That timber always looked like it was in deep shadow anyway. Longarm wished he had not left his trusty Ingersoll watch at home in Denver.

But then there were a number of things he wished he had not left back home. *Like his damned cheroots!*

He thought he was nigh onto perishing for want of a cigar.

And where the hell was Carter with the supply he had promised to bring up from town?

Whiskey and cigars aside, Longarm was beginning to worry that the scrawny Ranger was in trouble.

Longarm should have insisted that the two of them go down together, he thought. But then hindsight is always perfect. Forethought . . . not so.

He closed the damper on the stove, buckled on his .45, and went down to the horse trap to get the broad-bodied sorrel.

He put the bridle onto the big horse, led it out of the gate, and leaped onto the horse's back. He intended to go find Carter while he still had a little daylight left.It was fully night by the time Longarm got down off the mountain following what by now was a clear trail beside the thin run of creek. He had seen nothing more interesting than a herd of elk he disturbed at their evening drink.

Ahead another couple miles he could see the winking lights of Good Hope. Now that he was down onto more or less flat ground, he let the sorrel walk a little faster. He had barely gotten into the increased pace when he reined the big horse to a halt.

Something, some sound that he could not identify, had put his guard up.

Longarm touched the grips of his Colt to reassure himself that it was where it should be, then touched his heels to the horse's flanks.

The sorrel dipped its head and started forward again.

And Longarm stopped it again.

The sound . . . what the hell was it anyway? He could not . . .

"Short." The name was half whisper, half croak.

It came from his left, from the direction of the little creek.

Longarm threw his leg over the sorrel's broad side and slid to the ground.

He did not trust the animal to stand ground-hitched, so he led it behind him as he moved in the direction of the sound.

"Don? Is that you, Boss?"

"Here. I . . . Oh, jeez . . . over here."

Longarm followed the sound to the creek, where he found Don Carter lying next to the water. Longarm could not see the little man very well in the darkness. He did not have to. The man's pain was plain enough in the rasping sound of his voice.

Longarm knelt beside him. "What happened, Don?"

"Ambush." Carter wheezed a few times, gathering both strength and breath.

"How bad are you hurt?"

"Less . . . than the bastards . . . intended. I'll be all right. Just . . . stopped for a drink. Feeling better already."

"You walked out here from town?"

"Huh. Crawled. Horse went down. Fell on my leg. They must have . . . oh, damn that hurts . . . must have thought they killed me. Heard them laugh and run away."

"They didn't ride?" Longarm asked.

Carter shook his head. "Ran. On foot. Had a hell of a time getting out from under that horse. Leg isn't working very well. Don't think it's broken, but tomorrow I'll be black-and-blue from my hip to my boot tops."

"I'll give you a few minutes to rest some more, then put you up on this animal. I'll get you up to the cabin and put your ass to bed."

"No. I want . . . jeez, this hurts . . . want to go back to town. Find that sorry excuse for a town marshal Stonecipher. Report this."

"You can report it later," Longarm said, "for all the good it will do. Which I don't expect to be very much. Not when you accuse Kyle Burgen of bein' behind it."

"No, but I want to report it," Carter said.

"An' so you shall. But not tonight. Right now I want to get

you back up to your place. You need to get ready for what they'll do next. Which I suspect will be to come at me in the morning. Don't forget, Burgen likely thinks you're dead now. An' after that last raid, when they got all shot up, he won't know it wasn't you doing the shooting. He likely thinks he has me bought off, like he offered when I seen him in town. He asked me to just not fire when his men came. Well, there was only one gun firing at them that night."

Longarm paused, bent low, and cupped a handful of water. He took a drink, then said, "I'm thinking Burgen will send one of his boys or maybe all of them, but they won't be expecting any trouble tomorrow. I'm also thinking he'll want to tell me to come down to town so's he can pay me what he promised." Longarm grunted. "I wouldn't trust the son of a bitch to honor his word even if I had agreed to take his bribe. Wouldn't surprise me if his boys intend to shoot me in the back on the way down to town so's there won't be a witness left against him."

Carter was silent for a moment, then he said, "All right. But there is no way I can get up onto that horse."

"Don't you be worryin'. I'll get you up there or tote you on my back the whole way up." He chuckled. "An' I damn sure don't want to do that. Now brace yourself. I'm gonna pick you up an' set you onto this here horse. Lay on him an' grab hold o' his mane. I'll lead him back up to the cabin."

Chapter 27

Longarm placed Carter on the bunk and stripped off what was left of his city clothes. They had mostly been worn to tatters as he tried to crawl home. His boots were about the only garments that survived intact, and they were scraped past the coloring dye on the toes.

"It's a shame you wasn't wearing some o' those big-rowel Texas spurs," Longarm said as he was again stoking the stove to heat that same pot of leftover coffee. At least this time he had some live coals to build on.

"Spurs?" Carter asked. "Why the hell spurs?"

Longarm grinned. "'Cause I coulda turned you onto your back, took you up by the collar, an' just rolled you back up the mountain."

"You are a very strange man," Carter said accusingly.

"Yeah, that's been said before. You got any laudanum in this house?"

"No. I bought you a bottle of that rye whiskey you like so much, but it broke when the horse went down."

"The broken glass must've been where you got that cut on your hip."

"I'm cut? I never noticed."

"Just another hurt amongst a whole heap o' them," Longarm said. "Wasn't real bad to begin with and it's quit bleedin' now. Damn shame about that whiskey though. Did you remember to get seegars?"

"Yes. They were in my coat, but I'm afraid I tore the arms off the coat and used the cloth to pad my knees. That worked for a mile or so."

"What about the rest of the coat?"

"I threw it away. Sorry."

"Damn."

"What do you intend now?" Carter asked.

"Now I think the both of us need to get us a good night's sleep. Those rannies won't be coming up here until morning. No need for them to, as they don't figure they need to sneak up and only expect to find one man up here. So we should sleep sound tonight and lay for them come morning."

"I hope you are right about that," Carter said.

"Yeah," Longarm agreed. "So do I. Think you can drink this coffee while you're laying down or d'you want me to set you up so's you can drink it?" Without waiting for an answer, Longarm scooped an arm under Carter's shoulders and lifted him into a sitting position on the side of the bed. "While you're more or less upright, let me fry up some fatback. We'll both eat an' drink an' make merry for tomorrow we may die." He laughed. "Isn't that how them old Roman gladiators put it?"

"I believe it is, yes," Carter said. "But if it's all the same to you, I think it would be better if the other son of a bitch does the dying. Isn't that coffee hot enough yet?"

"Hot or not, I'll fetch you some." Longarm took a tin cup out of the wash pail, filled it, and handed it to Carter. "After we eat," he said, "I got a tale to tell you. You might not like it. Might be pissed off more'n a little for I've been deceiving you."

Carter raised an eyebrow, but he did not ask the obvious questions. Longarm had said he would tell him after they ate, and that was soon enough for what he expected to be news bad enough to make him angry.

Chapter 28

"Billy Vail's deputy? That son of a bitch!" Carter exclaimed.

"He woulda been here himself except for Mrs. Vail having that operation. He hopes you'll understand. Hell, *I* hope you'll understand. Only reason I didn't identify myself was because he said you'd get your back up and not accept any secondhand help."

"He was right about that, I suppose," Carter conceded. "But damn it all anyway, Short. I appreciate the help, though I hate being lied to."

"And that brings up another little thing," Longarm said. "My name ain't Short."

Carter's eyebrows flew up again.

"It's rightly Long. Most call me Longarm."

"Deputy Long? I've heard of you. Word is that you're a good man."

"I wouldn't know 'bout that," Longarm said, "but there ain't hardly a thing I wouldn't do for Billy. Or for his lady, come to that. And I'm sorry about fooling you, but he said it'd be the best way to see what the trouble is down here and can he do anything to help."

"I never told him I was having trouble," Carter said.

"Reckon it was something he read between the lines then. He knows you pretty good, I take it."

"We've been friends a long time," the little former Ranger said.

"And there's not a thing you wouldn't do for Billy, right?" Carter nodded. "Of course."

"Well, then don't be denyin' him the same."

"When you put it that way . . . what can I say?"

"Say you'll lay down an' get some sleep now, that's what you can say. Get that leg rested some 'cause we'll have to face Kyle Burgen's thugs come morning."

Carter nodded. He stood, obviously in pain but able to stand on the injured leg. He took two steps forward, reached the table, and set his empty cup down.

"Good," Longarm said. "You'll be feeling much better in the morning. Probably feel like shit, but better. Come daybreak, we won't have to be in all that big a hurry, I figure. Burgen's people will take their time comin' up here. They aren't expecting any problems what with you dead an' me bought off by their boss."

Carter snorted. "Won't they be surprised," he said.

"Forty-five-caliber surprises," Longarm said.

"Give them a chance to surrender, Short . . . I mean Long." He smiled. "It may take me a little while to get used to the idea of you being Billy's deputy."

"Hell, Don, it took me a while to get used to the idea too after he took me under his wing and hired me on. He taught me good, though. If it comes to that, when it comes to that, I'll identify myself before I start any shooting. I did that the other night, by the way. I hollered at 'em that I was a deputy. Dunno if they heard it, but I shouted it plain enough." He smiled grimly. "Once we get the bastards in cuffs, we can ask them where all that blood trail came from. How many got put down an' how hard."

"You didn't bring any handcuffs with you," Carter said. "I know because I went through your bag."

"Don't you have some?"

Carter shook his head. "Not me. I left the law behind when I retired and came out here from Texas."

"No matter. We'll think o' something," Longarm said. He thought for a moment, then laughed. "Looks like you left the law behind, all right. Just in more ways than you expected to."

"Out here Kyle Burgen is the law. The town marshal down there, the judge, pretty much everyone."

"This here is still a territory of the United States of America, and I am still a deputy U.S. marshal. I got whatever jurisdiction I damn well care to take, whether these boys like it or not. Whether Kyle Burgen likes it or not. Come morning we'll start to clue him in about that."

Carter smiled. "I think I will sleep very well tonight."

"Me too. Now, shut up an' lay down on that bunk. You wanta be well rested come tomorrow." He spread his blankets on the floor and blew out the lamp that was burning on the table, leaving only the glow that seeped around the edges of the stove box to lend light to the cabin.

Chapter 29

Longarm spread the grease left from frying salt pork, spoon-
ing the hot and aromatic grease onto another of Don Carter's
sourdough hotcakes. This would be . . . He thought back but
was not sure just how many he had already tucked in behind
his belt. The cakes were past tasty. He sliced off a piece of
the pork, speared it with his fork, and added a ragged bit of
pancake to the fork before he shoveled it in.

"How's your leg?" he asked between mouthfuls.

"Middling," Carter told him, sitting down to his own stack
of cakes. "It won't slow me down when the time comes."

Longarm nodded. He understood what Carter was saying. When a man gets into a life-or-death gunfight, all other
hurts tend to go away until the critical fight is ended. Longarm had seen men with broken legs run a half mile without
ever noticing their injury.

Of course the other side of that coin was that some men
simply folded up at the first sight of trouble. He had known
criminals to surrender at the first sound of a bullet zipping
past their ear, while others might fight on until there was no
blood remaining in their bodies. Burgen's men could fall on
either end of that scale.

"You'll do fine," he told Carter. "You might want to pick you a spot that won't require much movement. If you don't mind me making a suggestion, I was thinking it might be a good idea was you to set up shop behind that pile of discarded rock up above the house here. I'll wait inside until they call me out to them. Which I figure they'll do once they get up here.

"You can take one of the Winchesters and a box of cartridges for it, then set up there and keep an eye on things without being seen. I'll try and take them as prisoners, but if that don't work out, you'll be in position to cut down on them."

"That puts you in the most danger, Longarm. This is my fight, after all. I should be the one down here close to them when they come."

"Shit, Don," Longarm said, "far as they know you're already dead. Let's let 'em think that just as long as they care to."

Carter seemed to think that over for a moment, then he nodded. "All right. That makes sense. But I think you should carry one of the shotguns when you step outside." He chuckled. "There's nothing like the look of a pair of scattergun tubes staring at a man's belly to make him slow down and think the inside of a jail cell might not look so bad after all."

Longarm laughed. "I think we been to the same school, Don."

"I agree. Now, since you are spry on your legs, Longarm, can you grab that coffeepot and pour me a cup?"

Chapter 30

Longarm was wrong. He had expected Burgen's people to sit on their horses and call him outside for his reward, then put a bullet in his back on their way down the mountain. Apparently Kyle Burgen did not want to bother with such niceties.

The men—two of them—came up out of the aspens, one of them carrying a lighted pine-knot torch. One took up position below the cabin door and somewhat to the side, obviously there with the idea of gunning Longarm down when he came running out of a burning cabin. The second man rode around to the back of the structure with his torch in hand.

The retired Texas Ranger did not wait for Longarm to discover his error. Don Carter took careful aim and shot the torch bearer in the back. The man fell from his mount, taking the torch harmlessly to the ground with him. Then before Longarm could figure out what was happening and make his own adjustments, Carter shot the other man out of the saddle as well.

"You can come out now, Longarm," Carter called down from the rifle nest he had made for himself a dozen yards uphill from the cabin. "I got both the sons of bitches."

Longarm stepped outside and looked up the hill to where Carter was pointing toward the one who had been posted ready to murder Custis Short when he ran out of a burning cabin.

"Check that one," Carter shouted as he rose from hiding and started down toward the one who had been carrying the torch.

Longarm did as he was asked. Burgen's man was still alive but just barely so. Bloody froth was bubbling out of a gaping hole blown out of his chest, suggesting that Carter's bullet had gone in his back and come out of the front, and more blood was dribbling from the corner of his mouth.

"You're done for, partner," Longarm told him, kneeling at his side. "Is there anything you want to say? Anybody you want told?"

The would-be killer steeled himself against a jolt of pain, then struggled to get breath enough to speak. "F-fuck you," he whispered.

Longarm smiled benignly. "God, I hope so," he said. "Next chance I get to get laid. But thank you for thinking of me. So what's your name and who sent you up here to die like this?"

But he was asking those questions of a dead man. He stood and gathered the reins of the man's horse, then walked the animal around to the back of the cabin, where he collected the other horse too and led both down to the fenced trap, stripped their saddles off, and turned them in with Carter's sole remaining sorrel.

When he returned to the hillside where the second killer lay, Carter was sitting cross-legged on the ground beside the man.

"This one is still alive," Longarm observed.

"Oh, yes," Carter said cheerfully. "But I blew a couple inches of spine out of the bastard's belly. Why, he just might recover and spend many years in Leavenworth or possibly the territorial prison down in Yuma. Either way he won't be able to use his legs ever again." Carter laughed. "Just think how welcome he will be inside those stone walls. He'll be easy pickings for any convict who wants a fresh ass to fuck. Run away from them? Why, he won't even be able to crawl. Any sorry son of a bitch who wants a piece of his ass can just roll him over and take the plunge."

"You can't do that to me. You wouldn't," the wounded man said.

"Oh, but I can," Carter said. "And I will. Unless . . ." He paused there.

"Unless what?" the question came out more like a croak than a spoken sentence.

"Unless you and I have a nice long talk about who you are and what you are doing here," Carter told him.

"I didn't . . . I never . . ."

"If you lie to me, friend, I will see to it that you are put in with the worst scum in your prison. But if you come clean and tell me everything I want to know, I will ask the warden to give you protection. The warden at Yuma is a friend of mine, and I at least have a nodding acquaintance with the man at Leavenworth. Either of them can put you in a cell with someone who has found the Lord. Some prisoners do, you know. The warden can put you in with that crowd and protect you from the vermin." He smiled. "Your choice, asshole. Now, think it over. Let me know what you decide."

Carter stood and motioned for Longarm to join him. He returned to the cabin, added some chunks of aspen to the firebox, and pulled the coffeepot to the front of the stove to heat up.

Chapter 31

"D'you think he's telling the truth?" Longarm asked Carter later over a cup of coffee that had been reheated too many times. Still, it was better than no coffee at all, he figured.

Carter shrugged. "There are no guarantees, and he has no reason to be fond of either of us."

"But you think he is," Longarm persisted.

Carter nodded. "Yes. I think so."

According to the raider, whose name was Tom Flaherty, he and the others had been hired for the job by Maxwell Jeffords. Kyle Burgen had been standing nearby, and Jeffords went to him to get the money to pay them. But they were actually hired by Jeffords. Flaherty never spoke to anyone except Jeffords.

The dead man below the cabin was Fat Charley. Flaherty did not know the man's last name. And he was not fat.

Fat Charley and Flaherty had been among the four who tried to sneak up on Carter and Longarm for the night raid that had gone so wrong when Longarm cut down on them before they even reached the cabin. Longarm's shotgun brought down a down-and-out cowboy named Jimmy Fleis. Fleis was badly injured but would recover. Most of the blood Longarm found on the ground the next morning was that of

Paul something. Again Flaherty did not know the man's last name. Paul had died on the way back down to Good Hope. Flaherty, Fat Charley, and Jimmy Fleis split Paul's share of their pay.

The men had received a double eagle apiece, twenty dollars, for their bloody—and in the long run futile—efforts.

"What will become of me now?" Flaherty had asked in a thin, whining voice. "You'll talk to the warden for me, won't you? I've been straight with you, just like you said."

"Warden?" Carter said. "I don't know any wardens, so fuck off."

"But you said . . ."

Carter had just stood up and walked away without looking back. Now Longarm asked, "You really don't know no wardens, Don?"

"In Texas I do, sure. But I have no idea who anyone might be at Yuma or Leavenworth, either one. That is cold-blooded, I know, but it got the son of a bitch to talk to us."

"Oh, don't get me wrong. I ain't judging you about it," Longarm said. He smiled. "Just marveling at how good you pulled it off. He swallowed it, hook, line, an' sinker."

"He wanted to believe it, that's all," Carter said. "He talked himself into thinking it would be so. And, hell, once he is sentenced and sent off to wherever, I might go ahead and write a letter to the warden there and explain things. Otherwise the poor bastard really will be sucking convicts' dicks and getting his asshole reamed wide enough to take a fire hose without even greasing it up."

"You're a hard man, Don."

"I was in a business where you either learn to toughen up or else get out. Or get dead. You'll notice I did neither of those things. Someday you should get Billy to talk about the things we did back then."

"I've heard some," Longarm said. "Looks like he skipped some of his Ranger yarns though."

"As soon as you finish that coffee, we can haul Flaherty

and the dead one on down to town. Turn them both over to Stonecipher."

"What's the story with the marshal down there?" Longarm asked.

"Heath Stonecipher knows how to be a lawman. He just can't be one, not with Kyle Burden pulling his strings about everything. I think Heath considers himself mostly retired from real law enforcement. All he wants to do is keep a lid on things. And keep Kyle happy."

"And the judge?"

Carter shrugged. "Ed Lowry does whatever Kyle Burgen wants, the same as almost everyone down there."

"Not to change the subject or anything," Longarm said, "but how exactly are we going to get the trash down to town?"

"I'm thinking we can build a travois for the two thugs. They can both ride in it. We can pull it with my horse. You and me can ride those saddle horses Flaherty and Fat Charley came up on."

Longarm nodded. "Just what I had in mind too." He grinned. "'Cept for the travois part. I was gonna lash 'em both over the back o' that sorrel of yours and let 'em ride belly-down that way."

"You're a hard man yourself, Long." Carter stood and hitched up his britches. "Let's finish up here. then go out and put the travois together."

Longarm drained off the last of the stout coffee, then stood. "Ready when you are, Don."

Chapter 32

Half an hour of work with ax and twine had the travois built. Carter and Longarm working together hauled Tom Flaherty to it and laid him on the bed of short aspen branches across the drag poles.

"This isn't so bad," Flaherty said. "Just be careful with the bumps and I'll be fine."

"You bein' fine ain't one of the things we're worried about," Longarm told him, "so shut your mouth, you murderin' son of a bitch."

When they dumped Fat Charley onto the travois platform with him, Flaherty set up a howl. Carter kicked him in the head and snarled, "We can take you down dead as easy as alive." Longarm did not know if the man meant that. But Flaherty certainly believed that he did. The would-be assassin shut his mouth for the entire, and very bumpy, ride down the mountain.

It was the middle of the afternoon before they drew rein outside town marshal Heath Stonecipher's office. Both Carter and Longarm dismounted and tied the three horses to a hitch rail on the street.

Stonecipher was seated at his desk reading a newspaper.

He looked up when Carter and Longarm entered. "We have a customer for you, Marshal," Longarm said.

"How's that?"

"Couple fellows tried to burn us out this morning. One of them needs the borrow of one o' your jail cells. The other one needs whoever does your buryin'."

"What will be the charge against the one you claim tried to set fire to your place? You do understand, I hope, that anything up at Mr. Carter's mine is out of my jurisdiction. And why are you the complaining witness here anyway, Mr. Short?"

Longarm dug his badge out of his overalls and laid it onto Stonecipher's desk. "I'm the complainin' witness because I'm the one placing a federal hold on the man. The charge is assault on a federal officer."

"You never said . . ."

"There was a reason why I didn't. Reckon you might understand that, Marshal. Now." Longarm cleared his throat. "You're in a tough spot here, Stonecipher. I suspect you're a pretty good man. Got your hands tied, though. Well now you need to decide where you'll stand."

"What do you mean by that, Deputy?" he said after examining the badge and handing it back.

"What I mean is that me an' this used-to-be Texas Ranger, who I have deputized for the purpose, are gonna go arrest two more o' your good citizens an' put them in your jail too. Federal charge against them too, Marshal. Conspiracy in their case. Conspiracy to commit murder of a federal officer for starters. Might be other charges, but we can worry about those later."

"Would you like me to help you?" Stonecipher asked.

"That'd be fine if you'd feel comfortable to do that."

"Who will the other prisoners be?" the marshal asked.

Longarm looked over at Don Carter and gave him the nod. After all the shit he had taken, it seemed only fair that Don have the lead in this.

"Maxwell Jeffords," Carter said. He paused a moment, and a hint of smile flickered on his face. "And Kyle Burgen."

Heath Stonecipher turned pale.

"So, Heath," Carter said. "Will you come assist us in these arrests?"

Stonecipher stammered, "I . . . no, I . . . no." His pallor was replaced by a sudden flush. He pushed his chair back away from his desk and swiveled around to face the other way. "Don't ask that of me."

"Bullshit," Longarm snapped. "You're a officer of the law and there is lawing to be done here, so man up and do it."

Stonecipher continued to face in the other direction. He shook his head stubbornly and in a weak voice murmured, "I can't."

Carter looked more saddened than annoyed by the marshal's refusal. "I thought better of you than this, Heath."

"You don't understand, Donnie."

"No, I suppose I don't." Carter turned and headed for the door. Longarm lingered long enough to say, "If you won't help us make the arrests, then at least you can drag in the trash. Park him in one o' your cells an' take the dead one wherever he has to go. And be sure to leave the keys to your cells where we can get to them. We'll be back directly with two more prisoners."

Stonecipher still had his back to them when Longarm and Carter left the marshal's office.

"I'll bet that asshole Jeffords is in that saloon yonder. He'll be the harder one to bring in, I'm thinking. Burgen strikes me as evil but not violent. Not like Jeffords anyhow."

"All right," Carter said. "We'll look there first."

They were halfway to the saloon doors when Longarm faltered for a moment and exclaimed, "Damn!"

"What's wrong?" Carter asked, pausing on the board sidewalk.

"I shoulda brought some o' the money I got stashed away in the bottom o' my carpetbag."

"What do you want money for?" Carter asked.

"See-gars," Longarm said. "I'm damn near perishin' for a smoke. Haven't had a proper cheroot since I started this game."

Carter laughed. "I have money enough to buy you a cigar."

"I got expensive tastes," Longarm said.

"That's all right. I own a gold mine, remember."

Longarm chuckled. And led the rest of the way through the batwings.

Maxwell Jeffords was one of three men who were bellied up to the bar. His dog sat beside his ankles.

Jeffords turned to see who the newcomers were. The man did not look at all pleased to see Longarm and Don Carter standing there side by side. The dog, on the other hand, wagged its tail and came to greet Longarm.

Chapter 33

"Maxwell Jeffords," Longarm announced in a strong voice, "you are under arrest for assault on a federal peace officer. Surrender yourself now or suffer the consequences."

Jeffords looked annoyed but not worried. "That asshole is retired Texas. He's got nothing to do with federal shit."

"No, he doesn't," Longarm agreed, "but I do. I'm a deputy United States marshal, and you are under arrest."

The other men at the bar shuffled quietly away from Jeffords, leaving the big man standing there alone, even the dog having deserted him now.

"You aren't gonna take me anyplace," Jeffords declared.

Longarm said nothing. He palmed his Colt and strode toward Jeffords, the dog now whining and dropping to the floor as it apparently sensed the tension between its master and this stranger.

"You ain't taking me nowhere," Jeffords said firmly. "You hear that, asshole? Nowhere. But if you got any balls at all, put that shooter o' yours back in the leather and we'll fight this out fair and square."

Longarm said, "This isn't a game, Maxwell. It's an arrest. Now, surrender your pistol an' come with us over to the jail. You can get you a lawyer or whatever else you like after you're behind bars, but in the meantime you are under arrest. And that is as fair and square as it's fixing to get."

"If you want my gun, Short, you'll have to take it off me, and I don't think you're man enough to do that."

Longarm very deliberately cocked his revolver and pointed it in Jeffords's general direction. "Lay it down, Maxwell, on the bar there, and step away from it."

Jeffords stubbornly shook his head. "I won't go behind bars. Not for no man."

Even though he was already facing the gaping muzzle of a Colt .45, Jeffords grabbed for his own pistol.

Longarm fired and a split second later another pistol fired from somewhere close to Longarm's right shoulder.

Jeffords was hit by two 230-grain .45 slugs, one taking him high in the chest and the other striking him in the belly. He grunted, a distant stare coming into his eyes, and very slowly sank down until he was sitting cross-legged on the sawdust of the saloon floor. His revolver was still in its leather, untouched.

The dog jumped up and ran to him, nuzzling Jeffords's throat and licking his ear.

Jeffords smiled and reached up to pet the animal. And then he died.

"Anybody else?" Longarm asked.

The other patrons in the place acted as if they did not know the man who just died, the man with whom they had been drinking and joking just moments before.

Longarm glanced over at Don Carter, who by then was already in the process of reloading his Colt. Longarm waited until Carter was done, then he too shucked the empty brass out of his Colt and replaced it with a fresh cartridge.

"Now," he said, "let's go find that other fella who's needin' some time inside a cell."

Chapter 34

Longarm and Carter left Maxwell Jeffords's corpse lying where it fell on the barroom floor, the man's dog seated at his side whimpering and nudging the body with its nose. Longarm felt bad about that, dammit. It seemed a good dog, despite its asshole master.

"Where do we go from here?" Longarm asked.

"He has an office across the street from the city hall," Carter said. He added, "That has always seemed appropriate since he gives all the orders around here. Lordy, aren't folks going to be surprised to see the big man in lockup."

"Hell," Longarm said, "with any kind o' luck, he'll be fool enough to resist and we can shoot him."

Carter gave Longarm a sharp look, presumably looking to see if the tall deputy was serious about wanting to put Burgen down. He was.

They walked the three blocks to a small park, in the center of which stood the tall, narrow city hall building. Across the street from it was a three-story structure with a pharmacy and several small shops on the ground floor and offices above, which included a lawyer's office and something called Southwest Holdings, Inc. There was no indication what was on the third floor.

"Burgen is Southwest Holdings," Carter said. "He lives on the top floor. They say there is a bodyguard to keep people from coming up to bother the great man . . . or so he thinks he is . . . when he isn't in his office. Or just doesn't want to admit that he is there. We may not be able to see him."

"Burgen is an arrogant son of a bitch," Longarm said, "and he doesn't know his enforcer Jeffords is dead. Doesn't know I'm a federal officer either. I'd think right now he doesn't have any reason to hide from us, so there'd be a good chance we can find him in his office."

"I hope you're right about that," Carter said.

They reached the handsome building, far and away the finest in Good Hope, and entered through a covered doorway that led into a spacious lobby. Inside there was a side entrance to the pharmacy and, opposite that, the door to a surveyor and land sales office. A set of stairs curved up to the second floor and, above that, on to the third.

Longarm lightly touched the butt of his Colt, reassuring himself that it was properly positioned. He noticed that Carter did the same.

Kyle Burgen was not the sort to do his own rough work, but you never know what a rat will do once it is cornered. Some will fight tooth and toenail; Burgen could well be that sort.

"You go ahead first," Carter said. "You're the one with the badge, after all."

Longarm nodded. And started up the stairs.

Halfway up they met a scrawny, nervous-looking fellow with his graying hair combed over a bald spot and shoes that should have been thrown into the trash several years ago.

"Afternoon, Benny," Carter said as he moved to the side of the stairs to let the little man through. "What are you doing here?"

"Oh, I, uh, I had some business upstairs. Personal. You know."

"Yes, I think I do," Carter said.

The man called Benny scuttled past them and down the stairs. Longarm could hear him practically race outside once he hit the ground floor. "What was that about?" he asked as he and Carter climbed the rest of the way upstairs.

"Benny is what you might call our town toady. He sucks up to Kyle Burgen and scrambles for whatever crumbs the great man drops his way."

"You think . . . ?"

Carter nodded. "I think the little son of a bitch saw or heard what happened to Max Jeffords and raced over here to tell Burgen."

"So the bastard's been warned?"

"I won't guarantee it, but I'd say there is a very good chance that he has been."

"Shit!" Longarm muttered.

They reached the second floor. A dark mahogany door on their left had a frosted glass panel on which were painted the words EVERETT CRADDOCK, ATTORNEY AT LAW. On the right was a matching door with wording that said SOUTH-WEST HOLDINGS, INC. The door to Southwest stood ajar a few inches.

Carter nodded toward it. "Looks like our little friend was in a hurry to leave."

Longarm said, "Let's go see what kinda damage the little son of a bitch has done."

He led the way forward and pushed open the door without waiting to be invited in.

A slender, bald amanuensis was seated behind a flat desk, also mahogany. The fellow wore sleeve garters, a green cel-luloid eyeshade, and garishly bright red suspenders.

A much burlier man was seated in a comfortable-looking chair to the left. That one had a pistol under his coat. Long-arm could see the bulge. It was likely that Carter spotted it too, because the little Texan half turned to face the fellow, who was obviously a guard.

When the clerk looked up, he was smirking. "What can I do for you gentlemen?"

"Now, why is it that I think you already know?" Longarm said. But he played out the game. He pulled his wallet from the right front pocket of his overalls and flipped it open to display his badge. "United States deputy marshal," he said, "here to see Mr. Kyle Burgen."

The smirk on the clerk's face broadened. "I am sorry, gentlemen. Mr. Burgen is not in at the moment."

"Uh-huh," Longarm said, "and when do you expect him?"

"I couldn't say," the clerk responded.

"Mind if we look inside that back office?"

"I do mind," the clerk said. "Unless you have a warrant entitling you to search these premises, gentlemen, it would be good if you were to leave now."

Longarm glanced to his left. The guard's left hand had crept to the lapel of his coat, obviously ready to pull it aside and get to his revolver more quickly.

Longarm knew damned good and well he could take the man—he had to believe that about anyone he faced or else give up his badge—and he felt fairly sure that Don Carter felt the same. But there was no need for gunplay. Yet. Especially since it was Burgen they were after and not a pair of unimportant hirelings.

"Thank you for your time," Longarm said, touching the brim of his old and beat-up Stetson.

He turned and headed for the door, Carter close on his heels.

They had not gotten halfway back down to the ground floor before they heard footsteps on the boards of the second floor.

Longarm looked back at Carter, above him on the staircase, and winked. "That'd be a visit to the law offices of Everett Craddock. What d'ya bet?"

"We have a problem," Carter said as they reached the ground floor and headed for the doorway.

Longarm lifted his eyebrows but said nothing.

"There is less than no chance that Judge Lowry will issue a warrant."

Longarm laughed. "That's all right. I know someone that will." When they reached the street, he turned toward the post office.

Chapter 35

Longarm borrowed a pencil and message form and wrote out his telegram:

NEED WARRANT ASAP OFFICE COMMA RESIDENCE COMMA ALL BUSINESSES BELONGING SUSPECT KYLE BURGEN ATTN LONG COMMA GOOD HOPE COMMA ARIZONA **STOP** LONG

He handed the yellow sheet to the telegrapher on duty, the same skinny, half-bald young man who had been working behind the counter the last time he was in.

"You want to send this collect again?" the fellow asked.

"I do."

"All right." The clerk spun the piece of paper around so that he could read it right-side up, ran his eyes over it, and then looked up at Longarm. "This is going to a U.S. marshal?" he asked.

"That's right."

"What does a marshal in Denver have to do with anything here?"

Longarm shrugged, leaned an elbow on the counter, and looked away.

"I'll get to this when I can," the clerk said.

"You ain't busy. Get to it now."

The clerk hesitated a moment, then said, "Of course. Right away." He went to his key and opened it with a meaningless sequence of characters, then signed on with the Good Hope key location. He started tapping out a message:

REPORTS OF POSSIBLE TROUBLE ON THIS LINE **STOP** INITIATING TEST SEQUENCE TEST ONE TWO THREE FOUR FIVE REPEATING ONE TWO THREE FOUR FIVE END TEST RENDICK

Longarm smiled. He was not surprised in the least.

"Very interesting," he said as he reached over the gate that separated the public portion of the post office from the private area for employees only.

"Say, you can't come in here," clerk Rendick protested.

"Sure I can," Longarm said, pulling his badge out and letting Rendick take a look. "Now get yer scrawny ass outa that chair an' let me have the key."

"But I . . ."

"But nothin'. I read every word you sent and they didn't have a damn thing to do with the message I gave you. Now, move aside or I'll kick you outa my way."

Rendick hastily stood and moved to the side.

Longarm sat down at the key and quickly tapped out his own message to Billy Vail. When he was done, he closed the line, stood, and smiled at Rendick.

"You might wanta walk the straight and narrow from now on, son. You refusing to send an official message like that could be taken to be obstruction of a federal officer. You could get two, three years in Leavenworth for that, and I don't think you'd like it real well there."

Rendick turned pale and seemed to stagger for a split second, although Longarm could not be sure about that.

"If an answer comes in, son, be sure an' find me. Real quick."

"Y-yes, sir."

Longarm headed for the saloon, where Don Carter had said he would be waiting.

Chapter 36

"Nothing for me," Longarm said when the bartender paused in front of him.

Carter raised an eyebrow and Longarm said, "I still don't have any money. What I squirreled away is still up at your place."

"Oh, hell, is that all that's bothering you? I'm good for whatever you want." To the bartender he added, "Give the man a beer."

Longarm added, "An' a shot o' rye, please."

The beer tasted fine. The shot even better. Carter asked, "What next?"

"By tomorrow we should have that warrant. No, maybe two days. I figure Billy will wire a federal judge down here, then that office will either mail or courier the actual warrant. You know we'll have to have the paper in hand when we serve it. Burgen and his lawyer aren't gonna honor a telegraph message."

"I can't blame them for that," Carter said. "A telegram can be sent by anyone. We have to have the paper with the judge's signature on it, but then they must let us look. What did you ask for in the warrant?"

Longarm told him and Carter nodded approvingly, then

called for two more beers and another shot of rye for Longarm. "So we wait," he said.

"And watch," Longarm said. "If Burgen shows himself anywhere in public, I can arrest the son of a bitch. So what I'm thinking, I'll stay here in town. You go back up the mountain and make sure he doesn't manage to send any more raiders up there."

"Are you sure you can handle things down here by yourself?" Carter asked.

Longarm gave the little retired Ranger a dirty look.

"Sorry," Carter said. He smiled and said, "One mob, one Ranger. I suppose the same holds true for you federal boys."

"If I can't handle things," Longarm said with a grin, "they've promised me a real impressive funeral. With drummers an' everything."

"Well, in that case you can't go wrong."

Longarm downed his shot and followed it with a swallow of beer, then reached for the bowl of peanuts farther down the bar.

"If you don't mind," Longarm said, "I'll keep this horse in town. Just in case I need the use of one. Don't know why I would, but it don't hurt to be prepared. You take the other two up to your place."

"Let me give you some money for food and a hotel or whatever," Carter offered. He handed Longarm a twenty-dollar gold piece and gathered up the reins of the saddle horse that one of the raiders had been riding. He swung into the saddle, and Longarm handed him the lead rope of the big sorrel work animal.

"Should I come back down tomorrow?" Carter asked.

Longarm shook his head. "Day after, I'm thinking. If anything happens that I need you sooner, I'll send word."

Carter laughed. "You're a liar, Long. If anything happens down here, you'll handle it yourself. Or try to."

Longarm did not bother trying to deny the truth of what

Carter was saying. He waved a comfortable good-bye to the little man, then took the reins of his horse and headed for the livery.

From there, he figured, it would only be a very short walk to Eleanor Pride's shop. He could likely bum a bit of supper from her. And perhaps something more afterward.

Chapter 37

"Ma'am." Longarm nodded and touched the brim of his Stetson toward the middle-aged matron who was inspecting one of Ellie's hats. The hat, Longarm thought, looked like a large bird wearing a clown costume. He would have been afraid to put it on his head lest the thing shit in his hair, but this biddy was peering at herself in a mirror and cooing happily.

The woman sniffed, obviously of too elevated a station in life to respond to a common workingman, which is what Longarm looked like in his overalls.

That was an odd thing, Longarm reflected. A lowly whore will accept a smile from anyone regardless of station or status, but the hoity-toity will hobnob only with their own kind. He chuckled. That must leave them awfully lonely sometimes.

This woman dismissed Longarm's presence as if he simply did not exist—and for her, he supposed, he did not—and returned her attention to Ellie, who was standing there with a hand mirror so the matron could get a look at the back of the hat too.

"Can you add a veil?" the woman asked.

"Yes, of course," Ellie told her.

The woman sniffed again, tilted her head to again consider her look, and said, "At the same price? With the veil, I mean?"

"Yes, I can do that."

"Very well. I will take it. With the veil included. Put it on my bill and deliver it to my house."

"Thank you, Mrs. Garson. I can have it for you tomorrow."

"Not this evening?"

"Not with the veil, no. I'll need some time to get that just right." Ellie smiled sweetly, implying that Mrs. Garson was entitled to absolute perfection.

Longarm did not fully understand how Ellie could be so gracious to such a snooty bitch. But then he did not have to eke out a living in this community. Ellie did.

Ellie saw the Garson woman out, bade her good-bye, then locked the door behind her and pulled the blind. As soon as that was done, she was in Longarm's arms, her mouth on his and her body pressed tight against him.

"It is so good to see you," she whispered into his mouth. "Can you stay with me for a while?"

"All night if you'll let me," he assured her, a comment that resulted in a small squeal of happiness from Ellie Pride. "Will it cause talk if I take you over to the hotel restaurant for dinner? I dunno about you, but I'm near to starvation right now."

"Yes, it would cause talk, I'm afraid, and I need all the customers I can get. I don't want to alienate anyone. Like Mrs. Garson, for instance. She is the wife of one of the town councilmen." Ellie laughed. "She seems to think that makes her some sort of royalty. No matter, though. We can have a lovely time here, just the two of us. You say you are hungry?"

He nodded. "Famished."

Ellie took him by the elbow and steered him toward the back of her shop, where her living quarters were. "Come along then while I cook something." She gave him an impish grin. "Then later you can heat *me* up."

Longarm laughed. "That sounds like a fair exchange, m'lady."

Chapter 38

Longarm finished his coffee and leaned back in his chair. When Ellie stood and reached for his cup so she could refill it, he wrapped an arm around her waist and gently squeezed. She bent down and kissed him. While she was doing that, he slipped his free hand underneath her skirts.

He groped his way past ruffles and snaps and buckles until he finally came to a patch of tightly curled wiry hair and beyond that the slick, hairless flesh that guarded the entrance to her pussy.

Longarm stroked her lightly, insistently, until Ellie became moist. More stroking and she was slippery with her own juices. When her body was ready, he penetrated her with a finger. Then two.

Ellie moaned and pressed herself onto his hand, her hips writhing with her own pleasure. She became all the wetter, her juices running free now, her pelvis grinding against his touch.

Longarm added a third finger, then most of his hand, and pumped in and out of her as if he were fucking her. Ellie cried out and fell limp against him. She seemed very close to passing out from the force of her orgasm.

He kissed her and gently withdrew.

"Come outa all those clothes now, girl, an' let's switch to that bed in yonder," he said.

Ellie eagerly nodded her agreement and was almost naked by the time they reached her bed.

Longarm shed all his clothing along the way—but then he had less to get rid of—and was bare-ass naked, his cock leading the way, when he lay down. Ellie joined him, kneeling between his legs and taking his dick in both hands.

"Beautiful," she whispered, then dipped her pretty head and took him between her lips. Ellie peeled his foreskin back and ran the tip of her tongue around and around the head, the combination of her warmth and the wetness of her tongue arousing him all the further.

Longarm stroked the back of Ellie's head while she pulled him into the heat of her mouth. And beyond. Into the back of her throat. She gagged once and pushed down on him, taking him past the ring of cartilage until he was almost fully inside her there.

When she lifted off of him, she was smiling. And so was he.

"Nice," he whispered. "Very nice."

She bent and sucked him a little longer, until he was close to coming. Then she released him, the air feeling cold on his wet prick, and said, "Not there. Not yet."

She raised herself above him, guiding his cock with one hand while she positioned herself, then swiftly lowered her hips, taking him into her body.

After the chill of her saliva when it was exposed to the air, the heat of being inside her pussy seemed almost too hot for comfort.

Longarm reached up, found her tits, and kneaded them, rubbing her nipples with his thumbs while Ellie pumped her hips. She arched her head back, her hair falling down her back, tendons standing out on the slim column of her neck.

She reached behind her gyrating ass and felt for his balls, fondling them while she continued to fuck him.

The combination of sensations was too much to sustain. Within seconds he felt the rise of his cum as it shot through the length of his cock and spewed out into Ellie's body.

Longarm groaned and involuntarily grasped Ellie's tits hard, harder, his grip a steel vise grinding into tender flesh.

She cried out in sudden pain. But she did not pull away.

He could feel a series of contractions inside her pussy as she came at the same time he did.

Longarm lifted his hips and held himself rigid for a moment. Then he relaxed and let go of her.

"I didn't hurt you, did I?" he asked.

"No," she lied. "Never."

There were bone white spots on the flesh of her tits where his fingers had dug in, but she did not seem to mind the pain. She smiled down at him, and once more reached behind her butt to find his balls and lightly massage them, arousing him again, returning his cock to a firm erection without ever allowing it to slide out of her body.

Longarm smiled. And began again to lift himself to the occasion.

Chapter 39

Longarm woke to the warm feel of his dick inside Ellie's mouth. He was already hard, had gotten the erection while he slept. Now Ellie was putting it to use as she sucked on him.

His cum rose unbidden and suddenly spurted out into Ellie's throat. Longarm groaned aloud and opened his eyes to see Ellie smiling up at him, his cock still between her lips.

"Now that," he said, "ain't a bad way t'wake up."

"Get yourself up, laziness. I have time to make us some breakfast before I need to open my shop for the day."

He shook his head. "None for me, thanks. I need to get to work. Got to keep a watch out on the street to see that Burgen don't come up with something before my warrant gets here. I figure I can keep an eye out on his building through the front window of that café, so I reckon that's where I'll be getting my breakfast. I do thank you for the offer, though."

"Couldn't he have fled during the night?" she asked.

Longarm nodded. "Of course he could have, but I'm betting the bastard is just arrogant enough to hunker down. He seems to feel pretty secure inside that setup he's got over there, and I'm betting he'll stay there. Besides, if he runs from me, the townspeople will see. There's bound to be a good many that the man has run roughshod over. If he shows any weakness, they won't be so cowed by him. They could decide to go against him. His whole little empire could collapse like a house of cards. The man has to be scared of that. So no, I'm thinking he'll want to stay. He'll want to beat me right here. But I'm thinking he'll pretty soon try something." He grinned. "I just don't know what. Or when."

"Whatever you think best," Ellie said. She crawled up the bed so she could reach him for a kiss. He could smell the faint saltiness of his own cum on Ellie's breath, but her lips were moist and mobile, and if there had been time, he would not have minded again making the beast with two backs. That, however, would have to wait.

Ellie stepped off the bed and stood, stretching, her body pale and lovely in the early morning light.

"Damn, woman, you just get better lookin' year by year."

"Liar," she said. But she looked pleased.

Longarm dressed quickly, wishing he had his usual clothing instead of these farmer togs. Overalls and a shapeless old Stetson were not his idea of proper clothes. He buckled his Colt over the ugly overalls and felt of the pockets to make sure he had some extra .45 cartridges handy, then kissed Ellie good-bye and slipped out the back door. It would not do for the townspeople, especially the ladies, to see a man come out of her shop first thing in the morning. Something like that could destroy both her reputation and her business.

He made his way through the trash-strewn alley to the side street, then headed for the café that was close to the city hall building. It was early enough that there were few patrons in the place, and most of them were seated along the counter, close to the pair of stoves.

Longarm chose a table beside the front window where

he could see out to the courthouse, the street, and most importantly, to the three-story building where Kyle Burgen lived and worked.

A burly, very hairy fellow was handling the early morning cooking while a much smaller gent in white shirt and dark trousers waited on the tables. The waiter approached Longarm. "What would you like this morning, sir?"

"Steak, 'bout four eggs fried sunny side up, fried taters, maybe a biscuit or two. An' coffee of course. Got to have my coffee to get the heart started."

"Coming right up, sir."

The waiter hurried away, and Longarm settled down to wait and see what might develop across the street.

He did not have terribly long to wait.

A large man whom Longarm recognized as one of Burgen's bodyguards left the Southwest building and walked over to the town marshal's office. A few minutes after that, the bodyguard emerged again, this time with Heath Stonecipher. The bodyguard said something to the marshal, and Stonecipher headed south while the bodyguard loitered there on the street.

Stonecipher reappeared five minutes later, this time mounted. He reined to a halt beside the bodyguard and spoke to the man, then rode off toward the west, in the general direction of Benton Mountain and Don Carter's property. Of course it did not necessarily follow that the marshal intended to pay a visit to the former Ranger . . . but Longarm would have placed a sizeable wager on it.

The bodyguard watched Stonecipher out of sight, then returned to Burgen's building. Moments later he was back in view again, this time with a companion. Longarm had not seen that one before but felt he could pretty safely assume that the man was another of Burgen's people.

The two walked together toward the hotel.

Longarm smiled. Stonecipher was conveniently out of

town and two of Burgen's boys were looking for something. Or someone. Who, oh who, could they possibly be searching for?

Longarm got up from his breakfast, draped his napkin over his plate, and told the waiter, "I ain't done here, so keep this place for me, if you please. I'll be back in a few minutes."

The man nodded.

Longarm touched the grips of his Colt to satisfy himself that all was well.

Then he walked out into the morning sun.

Chapter 40

He found them coming out of the livery stable. The pair smiled when they saw Longarm.

"We been looking for you, horse thief," the shorter of the two said. That one wore a Remington revolver slung low on his left hip. The other carried a Colt. Longarm thought it looked like it had a small frame and was probably one of the smaller calibers, a .38 perhaps or a .32-20. The fellow with the Remington would be the one to watch, he thought. That one was likely the quicker and would be the one to start the ball rolling.

"Horse thief?" Longarm asked, more amused than worried.

"You should know that Marshal Stonecipher had to leave town on urgent business, but he deputized us to bring you in on charges that you stole Thomas Flaherty's horse."

"In that case I suppose you have a warrant for my arrest," Longarm said.

The two men glanced at each other. It was all Longarm could do to keep himself from busting out laughing. It was obvious the two had not thought about the need for a warrant.

"I'm sure Judge . . . what was his name again? Lowry?

Yeah, I think that was it. Judge Lowry. I'm sure he'd sign a warrant if Kyle tells him to," Longarm said and snickered. "But then I bet Judge Lowry would kiss Kyle's ass if he said to do it." He paused for a moment and added, "Just like the two of you do."

The big man turned beet red and began to tremble. The smaller one reached out and laid a restraining hand on his partner's arm. "He's just trying to piss you off, George."

"Well, dammit, it's working," George snapped at his partner.

To Longarm the smaller, more dangerous man said, "We're placing you under lawful arrest. Are you coming with us or not?"

"Well now," Longarm drawled, "first off, this ain't no lawful arrest. You got no warrant and truth be told you got no authority either. All this is is an attempt to goad me into a gunfight." He laughed. "Which is easy enough done, boys. All you had to do was ask."

His .45 appeared in his fist as if by a magician's sleight of hand. The two men sent to brace him turned suddenly pale. Neither of them had yet begun to reach for his own weapons and already Longarm had them cold.

"Drop your gunbelts, boys," Longarm ordered. "You an' me are gonna take a walk over to the marshal's office where you're gonna join Flaherty in a jail cell. Go on now. Drop 'em. Unless you think you can pull an' shoot before I can pull a trigger."

Both men reached—but for their belt buckles, not their revolvers.

Chapter 41

Longarm marched the hapless pair straight to Stonecipher's office. The door to the left-hand cell was standing open. Tom Flaherty lay inside, still on the pallet Longarm and Don Carter had made to pull as a travois. Stonecipher or someone had propped him up on an overturned bucket so he could see something other than the ceiling. He looked pleased to see these newcomers, then less so when he realized that Longarm had them under the gun.

"George, Bernie, what's happening?" Flaherty asked.

Neither George nor Bernie answered him.

"Up against the bars, boys," Longarm ordered. "Kick your boots off an' hold steady while I make sure you aren't packing anything that'd get you dead."

"I, uh, maybe I am," the smaller man, Bernie, said. "So don't shoot. I got a derringer in my boot."

"Do knives count?" George asked.

"Knives, guns, billy clubs, or brass knucks—any damn thing I might object to," Longarm said. "Shuck 'em all."

Bernie kicked his left boot off, the derringer skittering across the floor along with the boot. A boot was a popular but damned uncomfortable place to carry a hideout weapon, Longarm knew.

George contributed a folding pocketknife with a four-inch blade, plenty large enough to do damage.

Longarm collected all their weaponry and patted their pant legs, ran his hands under their arms and around their waists, then turned them into the cell with Flaherty.

"Get me a drink from that bucket there, will ya, George," Flaherty whined. "I can't get up nor move around nor nothing."

George grunted as if he were not particularly happy to be running errands for a cripple, but he got the water and held the dipper so Flaherty could drink.

"I need to take a piss too, fellows," Flaherty complained. "Hold the pail for me, will ya, somebody. Please?"

This the two hard-cases ignored him, and after a few minutes a dark, wet stain appeared on the front of Flaherty's trousers, his urine trickling down onto the floor.

In the meantime Longarm was seated at Stonecipher's desk, making out a record of his arrests. The Good Hope forms were not exactly the same as the federal documents that Henry was incessantly making him prepare, but they were close enough to get the job done.

"George!" he called out after he located everything he thought he needed.

"Whadda you want, asshole?"

"What's your full name?"

"Whadda you care?"

"Me? I don't care. But if you ever want to get out and walk the streets again, somebody'll need to know who you are an' what you're in for."

The big fellow grumbled but said, "George Anthony Walker."

"Thank you," Longarm said.

"I need another drink of water," Flaherty called. His cellmates ignored him.

"Bernard Hatcher," Bernie said without waiting to be asked. "No middle name."

"Thanks." Longarm filled out the paperwork as best he could, then folded the sheets and stuffed them inside his overalls.

"How long did you tell Stonecipher to stay away?" he asked of no one in particular. And no one bothered to answer.

"All right, where has he gone an' what's he gonna do there?"

Again none of the three spoke. Longarm made sure the cell door was safely secured, then said, "If the place catches fire, just speak up." Then he left, closing and locking the office door behind him. Longarm pocketed both the cell keys and the key to the outer door. If Heath Stonecipher wanted them back, he could damn well come ask for them.

Chapter 42

Longarm walked briskly past city hall and on to the Southwest building. He entered the lobby and took a look up the stairwell before committing himself to it, then took the stairs two at a time going up. Being caught in the middle of a staircase could be a most unpleasant place to be if someone intended to waylay you. Longarm knew because he had been on both ends of that game a time or two in the past and wanted no repeats here.

When he reached the second story, he found the usual guard sitting on the stairs up to the third floor, but the man, while giving him a hard stare, offered no move to stop him as he crossed the landing to the door to Kyle Burgen's office.

Once in there, he was greeted by the same clerk as before and by a man he had not seen before.

This fellow was a different kettle of fish from the big bodyguards Burgen seemed to prefer. He was slightly built, with limp blond hair, a close-trimmed blond mustache, and a wisp of goatee. He wore a suit with a matching vest and string tie. His shoes were shined until he could probably use the toes to look up women's skirts.

Longarm smiled. "You would be Lawyer Craddock, I presume."

"You presume correctly, sir." There was no answering smile. The man gave Longarm the sort of deadpan look one uses when playing poker. "Do you have a warrant to search these premises?"

"No, sir, I reckon I do not. And that ain't what I came here for anyway."

Craddock lifted an eyebrow but did not speak.

"I came up as a courtesy to tell Mr. Burgen that two of his boys . . . three of 'em actually, but one of those is old news . . . some of his boys are settin' on their hocks over to the jail."

"Mr. Burgen does not know them," Craddock said loftily, as if there were no chance his client could possibly know any lowlife riffraff of the sort who landed themselves in jail.

Longarm laughed. "How would you know who Mr. Burgen knows? Or if he might happen to know these fellas, seein' as how I haven't yet told you who they are?"

Craddock did not bother to respond. He merely stood in front of Burgen's office door as if guarding the man. Which of course he was, although not in quite the same way as the bodyguards were tasked to do.

"For what it's worth," Longarm said, "one of these two is George Walker. The other one is Bernie Hatcher." He laughed again. "And they don't especially like bein' in jail. You might tell Mr. Burgen that."

Craddock nodded. "I shall so inform him. Now you have delivered your message, sir. Please leave, lest I file papers to charge you with trespass."

"Oh, I wouldn't want for that to happen. Judge Lowry would get ever so cross with me, I'm sure."

"You take this lightly, sir. The law is serious business."

Longarm's expression became just as solemn as Craddock's. "Serious enough to get a man dead," he said. "You might wanta remind Mr. Burgen of that too."

"Is that a threat, Deputy?"

"Not at all," Longarm said. "But it is a warning."

He nodded politely to the clerk, then turned and left the office. He gave a warning look to the guard on the third-floor stairway and sidled his way down the steps as long as the fellow was in view, so he could keep an eye on him.

Not that he actually expected to be shot in the back here. But a little caution beats hell out of making a mistake with that sort of thing.

The air felt fresher and cooler and infinitely better once he was out of that building and onto the public streets of Good Hope.

Longarm went back to the café. The table where he had been sitting had been cleaned off, the rest of his breakfast cleared away. The waiter seemed surprised to see him. Longarm grinned at the man. "I may not be much to look at, but I'm sneaky mean. Now, can I have that breakfast you was thinkin' I wouldn't live to eat?"

The waiter rushed to comply, first bringing a cup of steaming hot coffee and then a mountain of food.

Longarm ate, paid for his meal with the money Don Carter had given him, and said, "Save this table for me. I'll be back to it. Count on that. I'll also be needing lunch for three later."

"Yes, sir. I promise you it will be here whenever you want it." He fetched a RESERVED sign out of an apron pocket and set it onto the table. Longarm nodded his thanks and went back out.

He walked down to the post office, hoping to have received a telegram from Billy acknowledging his request for a search warrant, but there was nothing. Just to make sure the telegrapher was not brave enough to risk a federal charge of obstruction, Longarm again stepped inside the gate and helped himself to the key.

TRAFFIC CHECK **STOP** ANYTHING FOR DEP U.S. MARSHAL LONG QUERY

It took only minutes to get the return: "NEGATIVE"

"TNX" Longarm tapped out, then gave the Good Hope operator a cheerful nod.

He called at the post office window also and found nothing there for him. Not that he was expecting anything through the mail. There had not been time enough for Billy to respond that way, but dammit, the man might have had the courtesy to give Longarm some sort of answer.

He was feeling a little miffed when he stepped back onto the street. His mood was such that he was almost pleased to see both Bernie Hatcher and George Walker coming toward him, freed from jail and fully armed.

Hatcher showed a satisfied smirk when he saw Longarm emerge from the post office. "You don't have an advantage now, government man. Last time you had the drop on me. Not this time. And I'm faster than you." Hatcher stopped on the boardwalk in front of a cobbler's shop. The man's hand dropped into a hook that was poised inches above the butt of his Remington .44-40.

Walker was a pace behind him. Walker seemed less anxious for this to erupt into gunfire. But then George Walker was a head-knocker, not a gunfighter. He would undoubtedly be hell on wheels when it came to fists or even that knife he had been carrying. But it was clearly Hatcher who was expected to handle gunplay.

Longarm stopped about ten feet in front of Hatcher. "Was there somethin' I wasn't clear about, boys? You're the both o' you under arrest an' waitin' the pleasure o' the court. Now, turn around an' go back to that jail cell like good lads, y'hear?"

Bernie Hatcher's response was to go for his gun.

Chapter 43

Bernie Hatcher was indeed a fast man with a gun.

Custis Long was faster.

Longarm's Colt practically leaped out of his holster. A lance of yellow flame spat from the muzzle, a small pellet of hot lead riding the sudden wave of fire.

The first bullet tore Hatcher's throat out.

Longarm fought the recoil. Brought the muzzle down. Fired a second time.

Hatcher felt a dull thump on top of his breastbone. Felt something crack and give way.

He was suddenly out of breath.

He remembered that he was supposed to be doing something with the trusty Remington in his left hand.

But . . . the pistol did not seem to be where it should be.

He flexed his fingers. Found nothing. Must have dropped the gun. He . . .

He was a little bit dizzy. And his legs were weak. He wanted to sit down.

No, he already was sitting, although he did not remember doing that.

Bernie Hatcher frowned. Something was wrong here. He knew that. But he could not remember what.

It was growing dark too. His eyes were becoming cloudy.

He looked up at the late morning sky. So very pretty. Very blue. Funny, he had not noticed that in . . . he could not remember how long it might have been.

He was tired. He wanted to sleep. He wanted a long, deep sleep.

Bernard Hatcher closed his eyes. His breathing slowed, then stopped altogether.

He fell back against the rough, muddy boards of the sidewalk.

Longarm knew he had made a solid hit on Bernie Hatcher. Blood was streaming down his chest from the gaping hole in his throat, and a matching, if smaller, hole had been opened in the center of the man's chest. Likely his heart had been exploded and he was as good as dead on his feet.

Before Hatcher had time to fold up and fall, Longarm's aim shifted to George Walker. His finger started to squeeze the double action Colt and the hammer began to rise, the cylinder rotating to bring a fresh cartridge in line with the barrel.

"No! Wait!" Walker screamed.

His hand jerked not toward his revolver but into the air. He held both hands high and shouted, "Don't shoot, Deputy, for the love of God don't shoot me."

Longarm's finger stayed its deadly pull, and he relaxed his aim at about the same time Bernard Hatcher slumped to the ground and died.

"Turn around. Drop your gunbelt," Longarm ordered.

Walker did as he was instructed. Longarm moved in close behind him and kicked the gunbelt away.

"Do you have your knife back?"

Walker nodded. "Yes, sir."

"Get rid of it. Slow and careful."

Again George Walker did as he was told. "I'm not giving

you no trouble, Deputy. Tell the judge that. I'm giving you no trouble."

"I'll tell him. Now get on back to that jail."

Longarm followed Walker step by step back to the town marshal's office.

Chapter 44

Heath Stonecipher was back from wherever he had fled. He was seated behind his desk. The cell where Walker and the now deceased Hatcher had been was standing open and Tom Flaherty lay on his pallet.

Except now, Longarm saw, Flaherty had been silenced. The man was dead, his complexion pale and mottled, his eyes staring sightless toward the ceiling.

"What happened, Walker? Was the great man scared Flaherty might talk and implicate him? Did Kyle Burgen order you to kill Flaherty?"

"I didn't do that," Walker said, marching into the cell without having to be told. "It was Bernie that killed Tom. Neither of us wanted to but . . ." Walker seemed to realize what he was about to say and clamped his jaw firmly closed, speaking no more while Longarm retrieved the jail keys that he still had in his pocket and locked Walker in with Flaherty's corpse.

Longarm gave Stonecipher a look of raw disgust. "I thought better of you than this, Heath."

Stonecipher looked away, refusing to meet Longarm's eyes. "I had . . . I had business. You know. Things to look after."

"Out of town," Longarm said.

Stonecipher nodded mutely, still not willing to look Longarm in the eye.

"You had spare keys tucked away someplace."

Stonecipher nodded again.

"You used to be a good lawman."

"I still . . ." Stonecipher did not finish the sentence. He steepled his hands and looked into them. Longarm could just imagine what the man might be seeing there.

"What happened, Heath? Was it money that turned you?"

The marshal of Good Hope, Arizona, looked up then. He shook his head. "No. I . . . I couldn't be bought. I haven't gone that far down, Long."

"What then?"

Stonecipher looked away. "Comfort," he whispered. "Easy living. No worries about figuring out what was the right thing or what was the legal thing. It was all so . . . easy. Just follow orders. Do what you're told and don't worry about nothing. Then before I knew it . . . it came to this."

"You know, of course, you can be charged with obstruction," Longarm said.

Stonecipher nodded. He looked like he had been clubbed with a hog mallet.

"Did Burgen tell you to do this?"

"No," the marshal said. "He . . . he sent word. By one of his boys."

"Not Craddock?"

Stonecipher snorted and shook his head. "No, never. The lawyer knows how to protect himself even better than he knows how to protect his boss. The message was brought, and by now I'm betting that fellow is already away traveling on a nice, long vacation. Gone to Santa Fe, maybe, or El Paso. Like that. He'll be back in a few weeks after this thing has time to die down."

"Except you and me know it won't die down, Heath. Not

this time. This time it's for keeps. This time your boss is going behind bars and all his people with him."

Stonecipher looked up, angry. "He's not my . . ." His voice died away. "Never mind."

"Do I need to put you in one of your own cells, Heath?"

"No. I won't be going anywhere. You have my word on it." He sighed. "For whatever that's worth. I won't betray my badge." He paused and in a very small voice added, "Again."

Longarm nodded. "I'll take your word on that, Marshal."

Stonecipher looked up again. Longarm thought he looked grateful for that last bit. He still was, after all, town marshal of Good Hope.

"Where is Burgen now?" Longarm asked.

"He'll be in his office. I'm almost certain of it. He won't want to be seen as running. Not even from you."

"All right then. I'll leave you in charge here." Longarm smiled grimly. "But keep one cell open. Reckon I'll be needing it sometime soon." He turned and left the marshal's office for the cleaner air outside.

Chapter 45

"You know those three lunches I ordered this morning?" Longarm said to the waiter. "Well now I only need one. An' I'll want something myself." He sat at the same table he had occupied before, amused at the RESERVED sign that perched in front of his place.

"We have pork chops," the waiter said as if that were an accomplishment. And perhaps this far from good farmland it was.

Longarm shook his head. "Steak for me. Fried spuds. Biscuits. Just biscuit an' bacon for my prisoner though. I don't intend to coddle him."

"Yes, sir." The waiter nodded and brought silverware and then gave the order to the cook, a different fellow at this midday hour. Good cook, though, as Longarm discovered fifteen minutes or so later.

He was halfway through his meal when the cook left his station behind the counter and sidled over to him. He pulled out a chair opposite Longarm and sat down, leaning forward.

In a low voice he asked, "Is it true you've arrested Mr. Burgen?"

"No," Longarm said. "Not yet, but I'm fixing to, soon as my warrant gets here."

"What will happen to all the things Mr. Burgen owns here in town when . . . I mean, if . . . he goes to prison?"

Longarm hesitated for a moment before he answered. "I'm no lawyer, you understand. Anything I say would be more of a guess than an opinion."

The cook nodded.

"But he'd still own those things. Being in prison don't strip a man of his right to own property. It would take away his right to vote or to hold public office, but anything he owned before, he still would own. He could hire somebody to run things for him while he's inside."

"What if he was to hang?" the cook persisted.

Longarm gave the man a sharp look. "I don't have any reason to think that he would. Not at this point anyway. Is there somethin' that you know and I don't?"

"I was just asking," the cook said. He stood, replaced the chair beneath the table, and hurried back to his duties as the place was filling up with the lunch crowd from across the street at city hall.

Longarm could easily guess the sort of thing the cook would have overheard across that café counter, but none of that would be evidence. And it would take actual evidence, testimony included, to get that kind of conviction. With the U.S. marshals pushing for conviction on these lesser charges—and no real likelihood that state charges would be filed against the local powerhouse—the longest Kyle Burden was apt to be behind bars would be no more than ten years, probably less.

Conspiracy. Assault on a federal officer. That was likely to be about it, although perhaps Billy or the U.S. attorney could come up with something more. Certainly Longarm intended to push for as much as they could get against the man.

He finished his meal, collected the basket that would go to George Walker, and paid for both meals, making a mental note of the amount. From now on he would be turning his expenses in for reimbursement by the government. He was perfectly willing to lay out his own cash for Billy Vail, but he drew the line at subsidizing Uncle Sam.

Longarm headed for the jail, sauntering along at an easy pace but keeping an eye out for anyone that bastard Burgen might want to sic on him. If the man was willing to kill Tom Flaherty, one of his own, there was no reason to think he would draw the line at murdering a United States deputy marshal too.

Stonecipher was not in the office when Longarm arrived, but Walker seemed lively enough. Or at least he was alive. That would do for the time being. Perhaps, Longarm thought, the promise of a reduced prison sentence would convince the man to testify against his boss. There was a chance they could get serious charges against Burgen after all.

Longarm delivered the bacon-and-biscuit lunch to Walker, then thought it was more than high time he headed for a saloon. He was wanting a drink and a smoke and was not sure in which order those should come.

Chapter 46

Longarm stood propped with his elbows on the bar, one foot on the brass rail, and his eyes on the back-bar mirror, where he could see the batwings conveniently reflected. He had an empty shot glass and half a beer in front of him. Behind him a pair of sleepy-looking whores, probably just starting their day, were trying to drum up business from the few patrons in the place.

The first customer of each day was supposed to be a bell-wether for how the rest of the shift would go. He wished them well, although he had no appetite for what they were selling. Eleanor Pride more than took care of him in that regard.

Thinking of which. . . . He smiled. Perhaps he should pay the lady a call after she closed her shop for the night.

Perhaps? Hell, there was no doubt about it.

A newcomer stirred mild interest when he pushed his way through the batwings and fended off the advances of a girl—she could not have been more than sixteen, but her looks were hardened by bad makeup and rough living—as soon as he cleared the doors.

Longarm recognized him. It was Kyle Burden's amanuensis. The fellow, in a coat and tie now instead of the sleeve garters and eyeshade Longarm was accustomed to seeing him wear, paused, looked around the room, and headed straight for the bar where Longarm was standing. He seemed rather shy in these surroundings. Not a drinking man, Longarm guessed.

He stepped up to the bar at Longarm's side and in a soft, low voice said, "May I have a word with you, sir?"

"Sure," Longarm said. "I'm always willing to listen if a man has something to say."

"May I be blunt?"

"Sure," Longarm told him.

"My employer is aware of the salary paid to a deputy United States marshal. A man who is very good with a firearm and can protect Mist—uh, my employer . . . a man like that could command a good salary in the private sector."

"Really?"

"Oh, absolutely," the fellow said. "An amount three times your current rate of pay has been suggested. With loyal service, that could even increase."

"You're talking a lot of money there, son."

"My employer would gladly pay it. For, as I said, loyal service."

"How much did Bernard Hatcher make?" Longarm asked.

"A little less than what is being offered to you. But then you are somewhat better at the job, aren't you?"

"And exactly what would the job be?"

"Oh, nothing strenuous. Collecting rents, mostly. My employer owns most of the buildings in Good Hope and virtually all the vacant land. You would collect those rents and guard them. As well as guarding my employer, of course."

Longarm grinned. "That lawyer fella warned you, didn't he, to be careful about names so if anything was to be asked in a court of law, the worst I could do would be to speculate about what you're saying here. That's careful. I admire careful."

"It is just my thought that such a position might be open now. Now that, um . . ."

"Now that Bernie Hatcher is layin' cold on a table someplace?"

The clerk shrugged. Longarm was sure he had been carefully schooled by lawyer Craddock.

"So what do you think?" he persisted.

"How long do I have to think about it?" Longarm asked.

"My employer would appreciate an answer by tomorrow morning." He waved to get the bartender's attention and in a louder voice said, "Another round here, please. On Mr. Burgen's tab."

The bartender nodded and started to pour another shot of rye.

"Reckon I can give your employer his answer now if he'd like," Longarm said.

The clerk smiled. "Excellent. You will accept the position then?"

"Actually," Longarm said, "what I'm thinking is more along the lines of telling Mr. Burgen to go fuck himself. Or maybe you do that job for him too."

The clerk's complexion reddened, but he was not a fighting sort, not even when he was insulted. He puffed up like a banty hen, whirled around, and streaked for the batwings.

Longarm stood at the bar laughing. And enjoying the fresh shot of excellent rye whiskey.

Chapter 47

Longarm downed his shot—damn, that was good whiskey—
and finished his beer, then walked down to the café, where
the owner was manning the stoves but the same waiter was
on duty.

"I didn't save your table, Marshal. You didn't say and . . ."

"That's all right. No harm done. I'll set at that table over
by the wall instead."

"Thank you, sir." The waiter bowed and scurried across
the room to pull out a chair and hold it for Longarm. Longarm felt like some sort of big cheese as he settled in and felt
the fellow push the chair closer to the table for him.

"Do you know what you want, sir?"

"Coffee. Steak. Fried taters. My usual, you could say 'tis."

"Yes, sir. Very good, sir. Coming right up, sir."

Longarm drank a cup of excellent coffee, and by the time
that was finished his meal was ready. He enjoyed a leisurely
supper, then retrieved his hat and paid, leaving a good tip
for the enthusiastic waiter. Nice fella, Longarm reflected.
Busy.

He stepped out onto the boards of the sidewalk and by
long habit carefully looked in both directions before committing himself to the open street.

He saw . . . what the hell was that down toward the
livery?

Something, he was not sure what, moved rapidly out of
sight into the entry alcove of one of the shops along the main
street of Good Hope. Longarm frowned. Rapid, unexplained
movements were always suspect and sometimes downright
dangerous.

This one . . .

He palmed his Colt, just in case, and held it low at his
side, where it would not be noticeable.

He turned and started cautiously toward the place where
he had caught that glimpse of movement out of the corner
of his eye.

The last bodyguard he had seen in Kyle Burgen's office
stepped out into view. He was holding a lever-action carbine.
Longarm could see at a glance that the rifle was cocked and
almost certainly had a cartridge under the hammer.

Longarm nodded as if giving a polite greeting and said,
"Does the muzzle o' that there gun shift toward me, fella,
you are a dead man. Let it down easy an' no harm done."

It was good advice. The bodyguard decided to refuse it.
Instead he tried to bring the carbine up toward Longarm's
belly.

Good advice but bad choice.

Longarm's Colt was quicker than the would-be assassin's
Winchester.

The Colt barked once, twice, then a third time, and the
fellow was driven backward by the succession of .45-caliber
slugs slamming into his belly and his chest.

The Winchester clattered onto the boards and the bodyguard crumpled down on top of it.

All up and down the street doors were closed and blinds
pulled over shop windows. Good Hope seemed to be shut-
ting down for the night a little early this evening.

Longarm's expression was grim. His jaw was set and his
eyes cold.

Kyle Burgen had gotten more than enough chances. It was against the law to order a deputy United States marshal killed. Longarm was pretty sure about that.

He still had not heard anything from Billy Vail about the warrant he had requested.

But, dammit, he was going to assume that Billy had gotten that warrant and the paper was already on its way to Arizona.

He strode purposefully to Stonecipher's office and took a sawed-off scattergun down off the rack there.

"What . . . ?" Stonecipher started to ask.

Longarm cut him off with a curt grunt and a swipe of his hand. He grabbed a pair of shotgun shells off the shelf, broke the L.C. Smith open, and dropped the shells into the chambers, then snapped the action back together and eared both hammers back.

Stonecipher was still gaping wordlessly when Longarm whirled and headed out onto the street, this time crossing the square and rounding city hall toward the Southwest building.

The outer door to the lobby was locked, so Longarm used the butt of the Smith to shatter the door glass. He reached inside and twisted the deadbolt, then opened the door and stalked inside.

A bodyguard—how the hell many of them did the son of a bitch have, anyway—appeared at the top of the steps.

The man had a gun in his hand. Or Longarm thought he did.

Longarm fired up the stairwell, shooting from the hip. The Smith bellowed and jumped in his fists. At the distance, thirty feet or so, the shot pattern opened wide, so there was no need for close aim. Even so, enough shot pellets found their mark to drive the bodyguard stumbling backward before he fell facedown onto the second-floor landing.

Longarm raced through the thick cloud of white gunsmoke and stepped around the spreading pool of blood that made a crimson puddle on the floor.

He turned toward Burgen's office. That door too was closed and locked.

Longarm raised a boot and kicked beside the lock, smashing the door open.

The same clerk who had delivered Burgen's offer of employment was at his desk, back to eyeshade and sleeve garters now.

The little man threw his hands high and shouted, "Don't shoot me. I surrender."

Longarm ignored him and hurried past, into Burgen's private office.

The place was empty. Longarm whirled around and charged past the terrified clerk again and out onto the second-floor landing.

There was no guard this time on the steps to the top floor. Presumably he was the one who now lay dead at the top of the stairs to the second floor.

Longarm dropped the shotgun clattering to the floor, palmed his Colt, and rushed up the steps toward the third floor.

Chapter 48

The entire top floor of the building was given over to Kyle Burgen's living quarters. To the left there was a closed door, presumably leading into a bedroom. To the right was a large open area with a Ben Franklin stove and several groupings of overstuffed leather sofas, cowhide chairs, and small tables. A large china cabinet was against one wall and a well-stocked bar against another.

Lawyer Craddock was perched on the forward edge of one chair. The man looked nervous. He was sweating so badly he had wilted his batwing collar.

"You can't . . . warrant. Where is your warrant?" he demanded. A squeaky quality in his voice made it more comical than commanding. Longarm ignored him for a fool.

Burgen was not in the main room, so he had to be behind the closed door.

Longarm wheeled to his left and kicked that door open too. His boot drove it back all the way against the wall beyond and swinging forward once more to where it would have latched itself shut again if the latch mechanism had not been shattered by Longarm's kick.

A gunshot sounded from inside the bedroom. Then another and another. Longarm began to regret dropping the Smith double gun downstairs.

"You want to live long enough to go to trial, Burgen? Or should I just shoot you down here and be done with it? Save the bother of a trial?"

A fourth shot sizzled through the closed door, sending a spray of splinters into the living room.

"That gun ain't gonna do you no good, Burgen. You can't stop me with it. Even if you was to put lead into me . . . which I doubt you are man enough to do . . . I'd still nail you square. So you decide, asshole. Either you surrender yourself for trial or I come in there and kill you here and now. It's up to you."

There was no sound from within the bedroom. Longarm stood half-turned so he could keep an eye on both the bedroom door and the lawyer, a breed which can be sneaky sons of bitches, as he knew from past experience. Craddock, though, seemed to have no stomach for shooting. The man might be hell on wheels in a courtroom, but he was not going to stand up against a man with a gun in his hand.

"Which will it be, Burgen?" Longarm called. "Prison or the fucking grave?"

Kyle Burgen's response was a pause. And then another gunshot, this one muffled. It was followed by the thump of a body falling onto the floor.

Longarm was surprised. Still cautious, though. He motioned to Craddock and said, "Go in there and see if you can talk your client into surrendering."

Craddock looked worried enough that Longarm was afraid the lawyer was going to break out into tears.

"Go on now, dammit," Longarm ordered, gesturing with the barrel of his Colt. "Go talk to him."

Craddock very nervously stood and crossed the room to the bedroom door. He leaned in close and very stupidly stood directly in front of the door, where a bullet was likely to pass if Burgen chose to shoot again.

"Kyle? Listen to me, Kyle. I'm going to come in there. We can talk. I'm coming in now."

The lawyer pushed the door open a little way and slipped inside.

He emerged a moment later, pale and ashen from what he had seen inside.

"You," he muttered toward Longarm. "He . . . Kyle . . ."

Longarm grunted. "Son of a bitch is dead, isn't he? The bastard was a coward. Went an' killed hisself rather than face a trial an' prison."

"It wasn't . . ." Craddock stammered. "He would not have wanted to be seen . . . by the people here, you understand . . . He was a proud man. Would not have wanted to be seen brought low."

"Bullshit," Longarm snorted. "He was just a sniveling little coward. He took the easy way out. But it was his choice, sure enough."

Longarm holstered his Colt and turned away, thoroughly disgusted. So much trouble. So many deaths. All for nothing . . . except greed.

That was the thing. Kyle Burgen had been a greedy little man and it ended up killing him.

Longarm left the third floor, still reeking of gunsmoke, and went down into the fresh, clean air of the outdoors.

Two days later Billy Vail stepped down from the stagecoach to find both Don Carter and Custis Long waiting for him, his presence tipped off by a telegraph operator in Prescott.

"Don. It's mighty good to see you."

The two former Texas Rangers clasped hands, glanced around a little sheepishly, and then briefly hugged.

"Mighty good," Billy repeated. Then he turned his attention to his deputy. "I have that warrant you asked for." He reached inside his coat and extracted a folded paper.

"Put it back in your pocket, Boss. There's no need for it no more."

Billy Vail looked confused.

"I'm sure Don will tell you all about it, Boss." Longarm stepped onto the stagecoach.

"Where are you going?" Vail asked.

"Back to Denver, where I got some proper clothes to wear. You can fetch my carpetbag along when you get around to coming back to work."

"But what about . . . ?"

"Don will tell you all about it." Longarm grinned. "Most likely make himself out to be the hero of it all."

"But don't you want . . . ?"

"To listen to you old farts sit an' tell lies? No, you two enjoy the chance to see each other an' catch up on things. Besides, there's a lady up there that I'm sure is pinin' to see me again. So if you would excuse me . . ."

Longarm disappeared into the body of the coach, pulling the door closed behind him.

The driver leaned down from his box, checked to make sure his passengers were aboard, and shook out his driving lines to get the four-up in motion. "Hyah, boys. Move on out."

The stagecoach lurched into motion, dust billowing behind it.

Watch for

**LONGARM AND THE
HELL CREEK LEAD STORM**

the 402nd novel in the exciting LONGARM
series from Jove

Coming in May!

GIANT-SIZED ADVENTURE FROM
AVENGING ANGEL LONGARM.

BY TABOR EVANS

penguin.com/actionwesterns

Jove Westerns put the "wild" back into the Wild West

LONGARM
by Tabor Evans

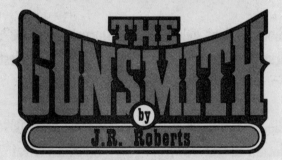

THE GUNSMITH
by
J.R. Roberts

SLOCUM by JAKE LOGAN

Don't miss these exciting, all-action series!

penguin.com/actionwesterns